HOMICIDE
for the
HOLIDAYS

Edited by
Diana Catt and Marianne Halbert

TABLE OF CONTENTS

INTRODUCTION

The words "Hoosier holidays" bring to mind certain soft-focused, Normal Rockwell scenes: sitting at the family table groaning from favorites—with sugar cream pie for dessert, naturally—and bundling up to choose a pine from the local tree farm or to drive down to the Circle to see the World's Largest Christmas Tree. (Shhh, we know it's not a tree.) Perhaps you've continued treasured family traditions, baking cookies to leave for Saint Nick or taking the kids down to the source—Santa Claus, Indiana, for what might be one of the state's best light displays.

You probably don't hear "Hoosier holidays" and think murder.

And yet here we are.

There's something infinitely cozy about a mystery story, isn't there? The more chilling the story, the better to keep cold nights at bay. Consider the Scandinavian cultures, which have brought us both hygge, the Danish concept of spending time in comfort with friends, and *The Killing*, both *Jolabokaflod*, Iceland's annual "Christmas Book Flood," the cheerful tradition of book-gifting and reading as a holiday pastime—and some of the darkest crime fiction out there. In cold places, apparently, there is no separation between the enjoyment of nestling in and the enjoyment of crime stories.

The Nordic countries don't own cold, or crime, as the stories within this collection will prove. It gets awfully cold in Indiana, too.

With the stories in this collection, the authors of Sisters in Crime Speed City Chapter might surprise you with the variety of ways the holidays can kill. This collection runs the gamut of ho-ho-homicide, from stories as sweet as a peppermint candy cane like Elizabeth Perona's "The Santa Cause" and Joan Bruce's "The Mysterious Mincemeat Murder," to holiday-themed tales as darkly noir as anything you'll find on Christmas Eve, like Ross Carley's "Hacked for the Holidays" and C. A. Paddock's "Into the Light Darkness Falls." If you're here for the crime, you'll find a Santa-cide or two, like "Killing Santa Claus" by MB Dabney and "Santa Slayer" by T. C. Winters ."The Reindeer Murder Case" by J Paul Burroughs and "Claus Santa: MIA" by C. L. Shore take turns at mysteries during Christmases of yore, while stories like "Killer Christmas" by Janet Williams, "Qraven" by B. K. Hart, and "Murder Most Merry" by Shari Held stretch the Christmas tale beyond the limits of space, time, and the grave. There's even a redemptive holiday theft, in "Unexpected Gifts" by Stephen Terrell.

The stories in this collection are gifts, homemade for you with love by Hoosier authors and wrapped, sparkling and ticking, little bombs placed under the tree. You'll find secrets, lies, twists, and quite a few red Santa suits stained with blood, as well as the recipes for treats mentioned within the stories. (If any of the recipes call for arsenic, that ingredient is *optional*.) The Sisters and Misters of the Speed City Chapter of Sisters in Crime hope that you enjoy this little dish of Hoosier hospitality—and wish you happy reading all year long.

—*Lori Rader-Day*
July 2018

The Santa Cause

By Elizabeth Perona

F rancine McNamara rushed into the house of her friend Mary Ruth Burrows, sweeping a dusting of snow into the front hall with her. She hadn't knocked. Their friendship was long past the stage where they needed such formalities. The jingle of the sleigh bells attached to the front door wreath faded as she closed the door behind her. She breathed in the heavenly scent of freshly baked chocolate cookies wafting from the kitchen. It made her mouth water.

"I'm here!" she called. She unwound the scarf from her neck and slipped the down-filled coat from her five-foot ten-inch frame, stuffing the scarf into the sleeve.

"I'm in the kitchen. Get in here fast."

Francine threw the coat onto a nearby chair and hustled into the commercial kitchen that had served her friend well through her years as a professional caterer and now as a celebrity chef. But Mary Ruth did not look as relaxed as normal in it. She stood in front of the bookcase where she kept her treasured cookbooks and recipe cards, running her hands through her auburn hair as though she didn't know what to do next. Adjacent to the bookcase was the double wall oven with a coat hanger protruding from the bottom of the upper oven. On the tile floor in front of it, a still body lay next to Mary Ruth's feet. Francine was sure there would be a rational explanation for all this, but at the moment it eluded her.

She looked up at her friend in alarm. "Is he dead?"

Mary Ruth shook her head. "Passed out. I took his pulse. It's fast. One twenty. I knew you'd ask."

Francine bent down to confirm. He was very much alive. He was breathing and had a pulse, rapid as Mary Ruth had said. The face was youthful, though it was difficult to say how old he might be. Early twenties to late thirties, maybe. Very short in stature. She almost wondered if he were faking unconsciousness, which was causing his heart to race. "Who is he and what is he doing here?"

"Repair technician from Kris's Kitchen Repair, here to fix my oven. Said his name was Gar, but I noticed on the badge it was short for 'Garland.' Must take a lot of abuse during the holiday season."

"Have you called 911?"

"No. I wanted you to get here first."

"Whatever for?"

Mary Ruth grimaced, panic clearly visible in her hazel-colored eyes. "When he told me it was an electrical problem and he wasn't sure he could fix it, I threatened to kill him."

Francine stooped down and patted the technician's cheek, watching for signs he was faking it. He twitched but didn't open his eyes. Still, she wasn't buying it. "Anyone would surely understand you were exaggerating to make a point." She stood and noticed again the aroma of chocolate just pulled from the oven. She saw dozens of cookies cooling on trays. "What's he repairing? Smells like you're in business."

"It's the top wall oven. The bottom one and the stove are still operating." Mary Ruth got an exasperated look on her face. "Did your electricity go out late last night for a few minutes? I had that wall unit on self-cleaning mode, and this morning the door was locked tight. I can't afford to have an oven down, not at this time of year! So, I got online and watched a YouTube video on how to repair it." She pushed on the bent coat hanger. "It didn't work, and now this is jammed underneath."

Whole novels could be written of Mary Ruth's attempts at home repair, Francine thought. "And how did he get here?"

Straightening her flour-dusted apron, Mary Ruth avoided eye contact. "I called the repair service. The number I usually call rang to this company. I guess they must have bought them out. Anyway, Gar showed up. He said it was related to the electrical outage."

The jangling of the bells on the wreath could be heard once more from the entryway, followed by the door slamming shut. Charlotte Reinhardt hurried in, unzipping her bright orange down-filled coat. "It's colder out there than being on reindeer ma-nure duty at the North Pole," she said. She pulled up short when she spotted the body on the floor. Nonplussed, she unwrapped the plaid scarf from her neck as though the body were an everyday oc-currence. "This must be the reason you called me over. Who is he?"

"Repair technician," Mary Ruth answered.

"He's not dead," Francine added.

"Well, that's a surprise," Charlotte said. She pulled her arms out of the orange coat and laid it on an empty stool at the bar. It immediately slid to the floor. "When we find them this way, they're usually dead." She made a half-circle around the body, appraising the situation. "His ears look kind of pointy. Don't you think his ears look pointy?"

Francine nodded, but Mary Ruth threw her hands up. "I don't care how short he is or how weird he looks, as long as he can repair my oven."

"He doesn't look weird," Francine said, "but he does look like that short guy who played Santa's elf at the party you catered at Alice's house yesterday for the Make-A-Wish Foundation."

"Now that you mention it, he does kind of look like that guy!" Mary Ruth said. "He was so pushy. We had all those kids there, but he pulled me out of the kitchen and made me go sit on Santa's lap."

"All of us had to sit on Santa's lap, not just you," Charlotte said. Then she snickered. "It was funny when Santa said you could have anything you wished for if you gave him the secret recipe to the Hot Chocolate Crinkle Sandwich Cookies you served."

Hands on her hips, Mary Ruth sputtered. "The truth is, it *is* a secret recipe, and I'm not going to give it out. It was handed down to me by my Great-Aunt Jenny. Well, verbally, at least. There's something not quite right about the way I remember it, though."

"You keep saying that, but everybody loved those cookies."

She shook her head. "They're too pedestrian to win the state Christmas Cookie Contest. There's something missing. I've spent the last three days experimenting, trying to figure it out. But I missed the deadline. The cookies were due today at noon."

Francine knew Mary Ruth had wanted to win the contest. Certain "celebrity chefs" in Indiana had been invited to participate, and as someone who occasionally appeared on Food Network, she qualified. The winner got $10,000 to donate to a worthy cause, and Mary Ruth had been angling for the Make-a-Wish Foundation.

"You should have asked to win the contest, then," Charlotte said, "instead of asking him to bring you some surprises." She rolled her eyes. "That was pretty lame."

"I was in the middle of a catering event! He caught me off-guard and my mind went blank. I couldn't think of anything else."

Francine jumped to her defense. "We can always use a few good surprises in our lives."

Charlotte indicated the technician lying on the floor. "He never said *good* surprises, did he?" She checked her watch. "I would have thought the paramedics would be here by now. When did you call 911?"

Mary Ruth started pacing. "I know I should have called them, but I was waiting for you to get here. I was just explaining to Francine that Gar—that's his name—told me I needed a union electrician to get the oven door unstuck because he wasn't licensed to do anything electrical. But he said all we needed to do was turn off the circuit breaker while the other unlocked the oven door. So, I volunteered. I was out in the garage by the electrical box probably more than five minutes. He kept calling, "Once more!" Finally, I got tired of this game and said I was coming back in. He was on the floor like this when I returned, but I heard some scrambling before then."

Charlotte rubbed her chin in thought. "So what was he doing all that time when you were out in the garage?" She scouted the immediate area. "Where're his tools?"

The other two looked around. Mary Ruth shrugged. "Now that you mentioned it, I don't think he ever brought them in. They must still be in the truck."

Tilting her head to the right, Charlotte sent her wig of curly white hair slightly off center. "I can't imagine a repair person trying to work on something without their tools." She nudged Gar with her snow boot. He didn't move. "You should call 911 now."

The technician groaned.

The women all stared at him. Francine waited a beat, but he didn't move.

"Hello?" Francine patted his cheek again. No response. "Gar," she said, prodding him.

Gar's eyelids fluttered, and then he opened his eyes. He blinked a couple of times. Francine was surprised by how bright green his irises were. She wondered if he wore special contacts.

"Where am I?"

"You're in my kitchen," Mary Ruth answered. "You're here to repair my oven. And now that you're okay, you'd better get moving. I've still got dozens upon dozens of cookies to bake for my customers, not to mention all the pies that have to be done before Christmas Eve!"

Gar fanned himself with his hand. "I don't feel so good." He had a high squeaky voice. "Maybe I need a cookie, get a little sugar in me." He took in the surroundings. "By the way, who are you people?"

Mary Ruth huffed. "Don't give me that amnesia ploy. If you can't fix my oven, just say so. I'll need to get another repairperson in right away."

"Your name is Gar, and you're with Kris's Kitchen Repair," Francine said, trying to be kinder. She took his now outstretched hand and helped him to his feet.

"Or maybe," Charlotte said suspiciously, tapping one foot on the floor, "maybe you're *not* a repairman. Maybe you're the guy who played Santa's elf yesterday at the benefit for the kids."

"What about that cookie?" he asked. His face flushed a guilty red.

Mary Ruth took a few steps and snagged a Hot Chocolate Crinkle Sandwich Cookie off a cooling tray. She held it out to him. "Here, have one of these. You and Santa ate about a dozen each yesterday. We know it was you playing the elf."

"Yeah," he said, snarfing down the cookie. "I get hired to play those roles at Christmas time. It's one of the only benefits of being short." He licked the marshmallow filling off his fingers. "Needs something."

Mary Ruth turned to Francine. "See! Even he knows."

"But I really am a repairman," he added. "Let me go out and get my tools and I'll do what I can to fix this."

Charlotte closed in on him like a spider on prey. "Get your tools? What were you doing when you had Mary Ruth in the garage flipping the circuit breaker?"

"Uh, trying a simple fix that didn't seem to work." He made a bee-line for the door.

She grabbed him by the arm and swung him around. A folded blue note card fell from his coveralls and fluttered to the floor. "Wait a minute!" She snatched it up. "What's this?"

Gar tried to grab it back, but Charlotte whisked it out of his reach.

She unfolded it. "It's your crinkle cookie recipe, Mary Ruth." She handed it over to her.

"Huh," Mary Ruth grunted. "He must've searched hard for it. I had it stuffed in one of my cookbooks. I've made so many experimental versions I have the basic version memorized." She placed it on the counter and marched up to Gar. Though she was only a few inches taller, she glared down at him. "Is this what you've come to do, steal from me?"

Gar's eyes darted away. "I don't know how that got in my pocket."

"Is it just a coincidence then," Charlotte said, taking charge, "that you admit to playing the elf at yesterday's benefit, that you knew about Mary Ruth's Hot Chocolate Crinkle Sandwich Cookies, and that you showed up to repair an oven you don't even know how to repair?"

"That's not true," Gar sputtered. "Give me a chance and I'll repair it. Think about this—how could I have made your oven stop working? And how could I have known what repair service you would call?"

Francine leaned against the wall oven. "He has a point."

Charlotte pulled out a bar stool. "Have a seat, sweetie. We're going to do a little old fashioned cross examination."

He didn't sit, so Charlotte gave him a push. He sat, his hands fidgeting.

"I'll need to see some identification. Your wallet, please."

Gar patted his pockets. "I don't know where it is. I don't think I brought it in."

Francine was already headed into the front room. "I'll check the repair van," she called back to them. She put on her coat and zipped out the front door. "The repair van looks legit," she thought. The van was a giant advertisement for Kris's Kitchen Repair with a custom-made fancy vehicle wrap in red, green, and white. To her surprise, the van was still running.

"Must be a diesel," she thought, knowing some diesel owners let their vehicles idle rather than shut them off and restart. Although it also occurred to her that a motoring van might make for a quick getaway.

She lifted the door handle, found it unlocked, and let herself in. The heater was going and it was warm and pleasant inside. As she climbed up into the front seat, she heard a male voice from the back of the van. "Hello, Francine."

The hairs on the back of her neck stood up. Slowly she traced the sound of the voice to where an older man sat in the back. He reclined in a bucket seat that looked sort of like a sleigh. Surrounding him was wall-to-wall electronic surveillance equipment. The man had a Bose headset over his ears, which he removed. The old "Mission: Impossible" television show immediately came to mind. She felt like she had wandered onto the set.

"Who are you? H-how do you know my name?" She heard the shakiness in her voice and tried to steady her nerves.

His complexion was ruddy and his face was well-wrinkled, with laugh lines that deepened when he gave her a smile. He put a finger aside of his nose. "Please sit down in the driver's seat and close the door. It's getting cold back here." For whatever reason, his calm demeanor soothed her nervousness. She did as he asked. Discovering the front seat swiveled readily, she moved it around so she faced him.

She noticed that his hair was white, from the top of his thinning pate to his neatly trimmed beard and mustache. Plus, he smelled of evergreens, like he spent a lot of time in the woods. Knowing Gar had been the elf at yesterday's benefit, she was fairly sure this had been Santa.

Charlotte's voice could be heard through the Bose headset he was holding. She was doing her best Perry Mason interrogation.

Francine realized why he was not surprised to see her. "You knew I was coming out to the van. You were listening in on our conversation."

"While that's true, I also know who you are."

She stared at the vast amount of surveillance equipment. "What is all this? Who are you?"

"Welcome to the Naughty or Nice Surveillance Vehicle," he said, spreading his hands. "It's so much more dependable than getting updates from unreliable informants. No one has standards anymore." He sighed. "Now, when I distribute lumps of coal, I'm fairly sure it's a good call. We've been giving out a lot of coal lately. The White House is getting enough to heat the West Wing for the winter." He chuckled to himself.

Francine crossed her arms over her chest. "You expect me to believe ..."

"You can believe what you want. As soon as Gar completes his mission, we're out of here." He slid one of the earpieces back onto an ear and listened in. "Though that may take a while," he huffed. "Your friend Charlotte fancies herself a real pro at this crime solving stuff, doesn't she? Although there's no crime here to speak of."

"What do you mean, 'no crime?' You're trying to steal someone's recipe! And you're illegally doing some kind of wiretapping. Shouldn't you have a search warrant or something?"

"Don't go getting all legal on me. You're not so innocent, you know." He pulled out a tablet and swiped it a few times. "Let me check my list. You've lied countless times to Detective Judson, hidden things from your husband, duped a state senator...do I need to go on?"

Francine couldn't deny the charges, but there were circumstances that made each one justifiable. "About that last one," she said. "Charlotte had me duped, too, so it doesn't count."

"So, we'll just call you an accessory to the crime." His eyes twinkled. "And I only want the cookie recipe so Mrs. Claus can make them back at the North Pole. I'm not really stealing it! We're just trading favors. You heard Mary Ruth say she already has it memorized."

"Only because she's spent the better part of three days trying to figure out what's missing! She's hoping to win the state cookie contest for the Make-A-Wish Foundation. I would think you'd have some sympathy toward that."

"Oh, I do. I admire her philanthropic efforts. And I'm all about wish fulfillment. You could say that's my cause. But I agree with her about the cookies. One additional little spice could put them over the top. And I know just what it is."

"What makes you think you can figure it out better than a trained chef?"

"I've eaten a lot of cookies in my day. I can taste something and know what's missing, but that doesn't mean I can figure out the full recipe." He paused to stroke his beard. "Maybe I can enter it in a different contest once Gar gets the recipe out of there."

Francine was aghast. "So you've tapped into a repair facility's phone, diverted the call to your fake business, and sent a spy into the house to retrieve a cookie recipe because you know a secret ingredient that you can use to win a contest? Talk about having no standards ..."

He frowned at her. "You misunderstand me, Francine. What matters is that Mary Ruth asked for some surprises. And when you sat on my lap, you said you wanted to believe again. Well... here I am!"

She rolled her eyes. She was not buying this. "Last time I checked it was still a week before Christmas Eve. And if you were the real deal you could have just let yourself in her house with a magic key or dropped down the chimney."

He gave a maybe-yes-maybe-no tilt with his hand. "We all have rules we have to live by. In my case, I can only get into houses on Christmas Eve. And who has time then? With billions of presents to deliver in twenty-four hours? I've got to tell you, it's a logistical nightmare. FedEx and UPS could learn a few tricks from us. Although there's a bit of magic involved, admittedly." He grinned at her. "So, I had to enlist one of my elves to help with the recipe deception."

"It's still stealing! That may be an elf in there, but you, sir, are no Santa Claus!"

He shrugged. "You still don't understand yet, do you? Maybe you're not half the detective you fancy yourself to be."

Francine sputtered. She was a darned good detective. This was just too unbelievable. "I'm going back inside and help Charlotte grill Garland," she said. "We'll get to the truth. Just try and stop me."

"Wouldn't dream of it," he said. He dismissed her with a wave of his hand. For a moment she saw snowflakes flitting around her like a bad case of floaters in her eyes. She backed out of the van and shut the door behind her. She went up to Mary Ruth's house a little foggy. She couldn't remember what she was supposed to do. All she knew was she needed to get in the house.

She rushed through the front door bringing a bit of the snow in from the porch. The wreath's jingle bells jangled again as the door opened and closed. She smelled chocolate cookies and heard Charlotte and Mary Ruth in the kitchen. Then she remembered. "I'm here," she called. She pulled off her coat and tossed it on a chair as she hurried to find out how Charlotte was doing with the cross examination.

Charlotte sat on a stool at the bar with three Hot Chocolate Crinkle Sandwich Cookies in front of her. Two had teeth marks in them. The third was in her right hand headed for her mouth. She bit into it, chewed thoughtfully and set it down.

Nearby, a woman in her mid-fifties in hot pink coveralls pulled the coat hanger out of the bottom of the wall oven. "There you are," she told Mary Ruth. "Should be back in working order. Let me go out in the garage and flip the circuit breaker for you." She disappeared into the garage.

Francine stared at the woman as she went past. Her hair was tucked behind ears that were decidedly not pointy. "Who is she?"

"Repair technician," Mary Ruth said.

"But she used to be a he!"

"Are you saying she's transgendered?" Charlotte looked shocked. "How would you know that, Francine?"

"I mean, when I was in here before, it was a repair*man*, not woman. He was trying to steal your recipe, Mary Ruth. The one for the Hot Chocolate Crinkle Sandwich Cookies!"

Mary Ruth and Charlotte exchanged glances. "Maybe you'd better sit down," Charlotte said. "You just got here."

Francine drew herself up to her full height. "No, I didn't. I got here *ahead* of you. I was just out in the repair van, talking to…" She couldn't bring herself to say Santa Claus. "Just a minute," she said. She retraced her steps to the front room where she looked out the window. A repair van sat in the driveway. It was from A Woman's Touch Appliance Repair Service. She didn't remember seeing that.

She walked slowly back to the kitchen, thinking.

"This one," Charlotte said to Mary Ruth, indicating one of the three cookies, "has too much cinnamon in it. The second is a little bland. The third is just weird. I don't think the answer is tarragon."

Mary Ruth pursed her mouth. "I didn't think so. It was a desperate guess."

"I know he was stealing the recipe," Francine insisted. "Charlotte recovered it before he got away. She put it on the counter."

Francine scoured the counter looking for it.

The technician came back from the garage. "That should take care of it. We'll send you an invoice," she said to Mary Ruth. She gathered up her tools and left.

Francine was still mystified. "But you called us over because the repairman had passed out," she insisted.

Mary Ruth sighed. She handed Francine one of the crinkle cookies. "No. This is what I called the two of you over for. To taste-test for me. Though it doesn't matter now. Cookie samples had to be provided to the judges hours ago."

The jangle of the bells from the front door rang again. "I thought the repair woman left," Charlotte said.

Joy McQueen danced into the kitchen carrying a huge cardboard check, the type used for demonstration purposes at press conferences. "Look what I have for the winner of the state cookie contest!" she said. "The $10,000 we're presenting at the 4:00 press conference." Joy, a correspondent for the local ABC affiliate, was also serving as the volunteer Communication Chairperson for the contest.

Mary Ruth was less than enthused. "That's nice."

Joy placed the check on the floor and planted her fists on her hips. "That's no way for the baker of the Hot Chocolate Crinkle Sandwich Cookies with Cardamom Marshmallow Filling to act."

"Cardamom!" Mary Ruth smacked her forehead. "That makes sense. I bet cardamom was exactly what Great Aunt Jenny used. Wish I thought of it in time."

Frowning, Joy cast a puzzling look at Francine. "What is she talking about?"

"So, who won?" Mary Ruth asked politely.

Joy pointed to the check. "Who is this made out to?"

"The Make-a-Wish Foundation."

Joy bent over and took a good look at it. "Oh, right. But wasn't that the charity you played for?"

Mary Ruth sighed. "Yes. And don't get me wrong. I'm glad someone else won for them. It's just...you know..."

Joy's arms windmilled around. "I still don't get it, Mary Ruth. Why are you being so dense? Your cookies won!"

"But I didn't send any cookies! I didn't enter the contest!" She scrunched up her face. "At least, I don't think I did."

"Someone sent the cookies in. They had your name on them."

Joy, Charlotte, and Mary Ruth looked at each other, mystified.

"Do you know who delivered them?" Francine asked excitedly, although she wasn't completely sure she wanted to know the answer. "Was it a short guy with pointy ears?"

Joy thought a moment. "Actually, it was. How did you know? Was it you who sent them?"

The same chill Francine had earlier when she entered the Naughty and Nice Surveillance Vehicle and heard Santa's voice now spread from the back of her neck to the top of her head. She understood what happened. And why.

She turned to Mary Ruth. "You asked Santa for surprises, didn't you?"

Mary Ruth nodded.

"Well, surprise!"

And in that moment, just for a moment, she believed.

Hot Chocolate Crinkle Sandwich Cookies with Cardamom Marshmallow Filling

Use your favorite chocolate crinkle cookie recipe for the dough, or try this one Mary Ruth modified from King Arthur Flour.

Cookies

1 1/3 cups chopped bittersweet chocolate or chocolate chips

1/2 cup (8 tablespoons) unsalted butter

2/3 cup granulated sugar

3 large eggs

2 teaspoons vanilla extract

2 teaspoons espresso powder (optional, but Mary Ruth recommends)

1/2 teaspoon baking powder

1/4 teaspoon salt

1 2/3 cups unbleached all-purpose flour

Granulated sugar and confectioners' sugar, for coating

Marshmallow filling

1 1/4 cups marshmallow crème

1/2 cup butter, softened

1/4 teaspoon vanilla

1 1/4 cups confectioners' sugar

1/8 teaspoon cardamom (to start)

To make the dough, place the chocolate and butter in a small saucepan or microwave-safe bowl, and heat or microwave until the butter melts. Remove it from the heat, and stir until the chocolate melts and the mixture is smooth.

In a separate bowl, beat together the sugar, eggs, vanilla and espresso powder. Stir in the chocolate mixture, baking powder and salt, then the flour. Chill the dough for 2 to 3 hours, or overnight; it'll firm up considerably.

Preheat the oven to 325°F. Lightly grease a couple of baking sheets, or line them with parchment paper.

Using two shallow bowls, place one cup of granulated sugar in one and one cup of powdered sugar in the other. NOTE: Since these are being used for sandwich cookies, you will want to make smaller cookies. Scoop out about half a teaspoon portion or so of the dough and drop into the granulated sugar, roll to coat, and then into the confectioners' sugar to roll and coat. Place the cookies on the prepared baking sheets, leaving about 1 1/2" between them.

Bake the cookies for 10 minutes, switching the position of the pans (top to bottom, and front to back) midway through the baking time. As the cookies bake, they'll flatten out and acquire their distinctive "streaked" appearance.

Remove the cookies from the oven, and allow them to cool on a rack.

In the meantime, prepare the marshmallow filling. In a bowl using an electric mixer, beat all the ingredients together except the cardamom. Once incorporated, mix in the cardamom. Add a bit more if it suits your taste. Cardamom is a tricky spice; a little goes a long way, so taste each time you add to make sure you don't overdo it. Also, please be aware that this is a very sweet icing.

To assemble the cookies, spread a layer of the marshmallow frosting on the bottom of one cookie and top with the bottom of a second so that the crinkle side points outward on both cookies.

Makes 4 dozen or so sandwich cookies, depending on how big you make them. Enjoy!

Hacked for the Holidays

By Ross Carley

I f it hadn't been for the pale light from a scraggly Christmas tree on the coffee table, I would have tripped over his body. The acrid, coppery stench of blood engulfed me as I closed the drapes and flipped on the overhead light.

I'd found Rudy Nicholas, known to his acquaintances as Red because of his carrot-colored hair and beard, and to the international computer hacking community on the darknet as NikCrypt. He was lying on his back beside the sofa, a small-caliber pistol near his left hand. A head wound had stopped oozing. Blood was clotted in his beard and coagulated on the thin carpet.

Nausea and disorientation swept over me. My mind flashed back to an Army cafeteria in Iraq. The bodies of Schumacher and Wilson at my feet. Eighteen comrades dead. Dropping to my knees, one hand on the sofa for support, I willed myself not to vomit.

I breathed deeply until my vision cleared. Sweating profusely, I crawled to Nicholas' body. He reeked of alcohol and body odor. Vacant staring eyes on his mottled face and a lack of a pulse on his cool skin verified it was too late to help him.

I pushed myself to my feet, scanned the condo to make sure no one else was there, and pondered possibilities. The proximity of the nickel-plated .32 pistol to his hand gave the impression of suicide.

Or, he could have been murdered. His lifestyle as a hacker provided potential motivations. Fierce competition raged between criminals called black-hat hackers intent on bringing the internet crashing down, and good guys, the white hats, just as determined to protect it. There was also his alleged involvement with sensitive government projects. An enigma, Red worked in areas somewhere between a white hat and a black hat. Call him a gray hat.

I knew almost nothing about his personal life. Pat Acton at Maltrack, a cybersecurity company, had hired me to check up on him. Acton was concerned because Red, usually punctual with his professional obligations and a stickler for timelines, was late on delivering a software analysis module, a part of their new anti-malware system.

My calls to Red had gone unanswered. Twice during the day while I was nearby serving subpoenas for the Marion County Sheriff's Office, I'd knocked on the outside door to his first-floor condo. Nada. So, I'd waited until after midnight to employ my lockpicking skills.

Now, I placed a call to the Indianapolis Metropolitan Police Department. Two officers would be on the scene in five to ten minutes.

But, just as important to me was my need to reach out to my primary PTSD support, Tito Rodriguez. Tito was a homicide detective sergeant in the IMPD. He and I served together in Iraq in the military police and military intelligence, respectively, and we both returned with PTSD. I started to punch in his landline number but changed my mind. I had only a few minutes before the cops arrived. It'd have to wait.

I surveyed the condo contents, careful not to touch anything.

Three high-definition computer screens sat side-by-side on the table in the small dining area adjacent to the kitchenette. Two of the screens were off and black. The center one had a blank blue screen.

The table also held an empty glass, a half-full gallon jug of vodka, and a large plastic bottle of seltzer tablets, standing open with the lid beside it. Hacker diet.

Noticeably absent were work-related items such as notebooks, CDs, and DVDs. Ditto for cell phones and tablet computers.

A video cable used to connect one of the screens to a computer snaked across the tabletop from under the center screen. A black power adapter for a laptop PC also sat on the table, the plug connected to nothing. A laptop had to be missing.

Mindful of fingerprints, I used a paper napkin from the kitchen as I examined the power adapter. It was for a Lenovo.

A sudden noise from the kitchen startled me. Someone there? I knocked over the seltzer tablet bottle and dove under the table. Silence. Not a person, I realized, but ice cubes dumping into the automatic icemaker's tray in the refrigerator's freezer.

I took a deep breath. As I returned the tablets to the bottle, I noticed that something else had fallen out — a small computer thumb drive. I dropped it in my pocket.

At one-twenty a.m., the flashing lights of a police cruiser leaked through the blinds.

Corporal D'Amato strode into the room, obviously in charge. A short bantam rooster with black eyes, olive skin, and black hair cut in a squared-off flattop, his clipped speech was augmented by forceful gestures. After a cursory examination of Red's corpse, he radioed for an ambulance.

His partner, Patrolman Wishard, was tall and skinny, with a pink complexion and light brown hair. He looked vintage Hoosier and freshly minted out of the IMPD Training Academy. His serious brown eyes seldom left D'Amato. His demeanor resembled a puppy trying to please its master.

I gave D'Amato my driver's license and Wolf Ruger Associates business card.

He glanced at them and shoved them in Wishard's direction. "Here, copy this info."

Wishard's face brightened as he pulled out a tablet computer.

"Why are you here?" asked D'Amato.

I was careful with my answer. "One of my computer consulting clients asked me to locate this guy." I didn't mention that I was also a licensed private investigator using the business name of Wolf Investigations.

More flashing lights announced the arrival of the ambulance. Close behind was an unmarked car.

As D'Amato left the condo, he said, "Stay put."

He spoke briefly with the EMTs, pointing out the condo. He and the plainclothes officer from the car conferred briefly, then invited me out to the unmarked car. Both got in the back seat, one on each side of me.

"This is Detective Sergeant Simpson," D'Amato said. "He's taking over."

Simpson had the blocky build of a linebacker mutated by doughnuts. Thinning blond hair and eyes the color of muddy water set off a broad face with a sheen of perspiration.

"Start again from the top," he said.

"The company I'm doing computer consulting for sent me here looking for Mr. Nicholas."

"What company is that?"

"Maltrack."

"Racing outfit?"

The question took me by surprise for a second. I grinned, realizing he thought it was one of the numerous racing-related companies in Indy. "No. Cybersecurity."

After running through my narrative, Simpson said, "Let's go inside." Back in the condo, he said, "Walk me through what you did. Don't leave anything out."

After hearing my tale again, he said, "Looks like suicide. But we have to dot the i's and cross the t's. For now, it's being listed as death under suspicious circumstances."

He'd seen the blue screen. I kept my mouth shut. I needed to talk with Tito.

"You finished with me?" I asked.

Simpson glanced at his notes, then at D'Amato. "Anything else for him?"

D'Amato shook his head, then looked at me. "You'll get a call from IMPD if they have any questions."

∶∾ ∶∾ ∶∾

It was almost two a.m. when I called Pat Acton at home. I gave him a brief rundown.

"Anything you want me to do?" I asked.

"Yes. If I'm right about what I find when I pull some information together, Maltrack needs your assistance. Be at my office at eight-thirty."

My hand shaking, I punched in Tito's number.

A groggy voice answered. It was Carmen, his wife. I asked for Tito. Bed springs creaked.

"Wolf?"

"Yeah. Rough spot." 'Rough spot' was our code to indicate we'd had a PTSD episode.

"I'm going where I can talk. Iraq nightmare?"

"No, found a body."

"Tell me what happened."

I launched into an explanation, blurting out words until my tongue stopped working.

"Take it slow and easy. Breathe deeply. Wait a little, then try again."

Finally, after a few false starts, I made it through describing what occurred, trembling and perspiring.

"Is it related to your work for Maltrack?"

"Yeah, a missing persons case. Looks like suicide." My words were clearer, my voice stronger.

"Feeling better now? Think you'll be able to sleep okay tonight?"

"Yeah, thanks. I'll call you again after I think about a few things."

We were both quiet for a while. We always gave each other space at the end of a support call.

Tito broke the silence. "We're looking forward to seeing you at our holiday party."

"Thanks for inviting me. I'm looking forward to Carmen's Christmas cornbake."

"You're welcome, and I'll tell her."

❀ ❀ ❀

The next morning, I called Tito at seven-forty, on his way to work.

"You doing all right? How'd it go with IMPD?" he asked.

"Yes, and okay, I guess."

"What do you mean by 'okay'?"

"That's why I'm calling. Detective Sergeant Simpson seems convinced that Nicholas' death was suicide. Something doesn't smell right to me."

"So, what do you want from me?"

"Let me know how IMPD is handling it, and any details you're able to share."

"I'll do what I can," he said.

Maltrack was an international corporation with local offices on the north side of Ninety-Sixth Street, a half-mile east of Meridian. Julie, Maltrack's receptionist, had a visitor's badge waiting for me when I rang the buzzer next to the glass double doors.

After we shook hands, Pat gave me a Maltrack coffee mug and guided me into the break room. I chose a strong, black brew from the coffee machine that ground the beans and served a variety of beverages. Pat picked a cappuccino, then led me to his office.

"Wolf, we have a problem," Pat said. He settled into his chair and motioned me into a chair beside his desk.

"What's that?" I asked.

"It's related to the insurance policies we carry on our senior employees." He paused. "You said last night, or, I should say, early this morning, that the police were tentatively ruling his death a suicide."

"That's right. It's officially listed as 'death under suspicious circumstances' just to keep their options open, but the guy in charge, Sergeant Simpson, made no bones about his opinion that Red killed himself."

Pat sipped his coffee. "That's the problem. Let me explain." He cleared his throat. "We carry life and long-term disability insurance on our key people. That's to compensate Maltrack, and our investors, if we have to recruit and train a replacement. The amount is two-and-a-half times annual salary plus benefits, which in Red's case comes to just over three hundred thousand dollars."

"Red's been here quite a while, right?" I asked.

"Almost five years," Pat replied.

I had experience with cases involving suicide. "So, what's the problem? The benefit will be paid regardless of whether his death was accidental, homicide, or suicide, unless your policies are unusual. Almost all insurance policies have a two-year suicide window. If suicide occurs after two years, full payment is made."

Pat sighed. "As you know, our group in Indy was operating under a different name until last May, when we were acquired by Maltrack. At that time, life and disability policies for our Indy team shifted to Maltrack's insurance carrier. Each time you change insurance, the two-year window resets. If Red's death was suicide, our team is out three hundred grand."

I tried to look helpful. "IMPD is investigating the death as occurring under suspicious circumstances. That could mean anything."

"Exactly," Pat said. "That's why you're here. We want you to make sure that the insurance company plays fair. If it's clearly suicide, it is what it is. We need to know, regardless. We'd like to employ your services as a private investigator."

"Why me?"

"Several reasons." He ticked them off on his fingers. "We're aware of your role in recent murder investigations. You have connections at IMPD. Your references are excellent. You're familiar with Maltrack, and you're technically competent."

I shifted in my seat. Because of the holidays, my calendar was empty except for being on the hook to serve subpoenas, and my checking account was pretty thin.

"Okay, I'll see what I can do."

"What other information can we provide that'll help you?"

"Was he married? Kids?"

"No to both questions. But he went through a nasty divorce. His ex, Bonnie, is a computer analyst. I don't know where she's employed, but she's a piece of work."

"Did Maltrack provide Red with a laptop?"

"Yes, each of our employees has one. A Lenovo."

"Well, it appears to be missing."

"That's troubling, but not devastating. The contents of all laptops are heavily encrypted."

"I'll let IMPD know about it, though. I'm not sure they noticed it was missing."

"Thanks."

"And I found this." I dropped the thumb drive from the seltzer tablet jar into Pat's hand, noticing for the first time Maltrack's logo imprinted on it.

"Where'd you get it?"

"Don't ask."

"Okay, I won't. It's almost certainly a backup of his laptop. We'll decrypt it and let you know if we find anything interesting."

"Who were Red's friends? Anyone at Maltrack he hung out with? Women friends?"

Pat thought for a minute. "His best buddy was probably Ed Burberry. He's head of cybersecurity for First Hoosier Bank and Trust. Red didn't socialize with anyone I know of and said that he was finished with women."

"Okay, I'll start with Burberry. I assume you're distributing an email on Red's death?"

Pat nodded. "Yeah, it's already known via the grapevine, but I need to send something out."

"Please put my name and email in whatever you send. Say that anyone can contact me confidentially, okay?"

Pat knitted his brows and frowned. "Will do."

He sat back. "By the way, we just got a new piece of software we're installing today that might help us locate the missing laptop, but only if the thieves put it onto a network."

"So, if they keep it disconnected from a network, we're out of luck."

"I'm afraid so. But if they connect it, say, to use analysis equipment to try to crack the encryption, we might be able to trace it through its media access control address. We know them for all the computers we own."

"I don't know much about MAC addresses." I knew almost nothing but didn't want to admit it.

"A computer's MAC address is a unique identifier, like a serial number, assigned to the network communications hardware in a machine. No two MACs are the same, and they don't change with location like the internet protocol address."

"You said you '*might* be able.' Please explain."

"Sure. Maltrack can locate a machine if we either know what internet service provider they use, or we know what computer server is managing their local network. The new application not only finds the IP address, but the physical street address. It'll be operational later this morning. It's pretty cool."

"But you don't know either the ISP or the server, so right now you're up the creek."

"Right. See if you can find us a paddle," he concluded, smiling.

༄ ༄ ༄

I served subpoenas the rest of the day and scheduled a meeting with Ed Burberry for ten the next morning. His office was on the eighteenth floor of the First Hoosier Tower, a thirty-story high-rise on the canal in downtown Indy.

When people ask me what I do as a private investigator, I often answer that I poke around. Poking around Red's neighborhood to find out if anyone had seen anything seemed logical.

His condominium was in the Butler Tarkington neighborhood, and I hadn't had lunch or dinner yet, so I decided on carry-out from the Illinois Street Food Emporium. It's only a five-minute drive west of my Broad Ripple office, and I sometimes go there for lunch. I ordered a turkey wrap and a Diet Coke and used their restroom while I waited. I'd be good for a couple of hours until the soda hit me.

I parked a few spaces down from Red's condo in a good place to watch the nearby units and ate my takeout dinner.

About five-thirty a woman with bobbed salt-and-pepper hair emerged from a townhouse across from Red's condo, propelled by a black Labrador retriever. They passed me on the other side of the street.

After a few minutes I got out and started across the street, then stopped and straightened my tie. The wind and freezing temperature prompted me to put on my jacket. I might as well look official *and* be warm. I had my PI identification and Wolf Investigations card out as she and her dog came back.

The sun was just setting, and Christmas decorations were lighting up in the neighborhood, adding a festive note. I didn't feel festive.

She approached me warily. Her dog was utterly useless as a bodyguard since it was wagging its tail so hard it almost fell over.

"Hello. My name is Wolf Ruger. I'm investigating the death of Mr. Nicholas, across the street."

She fleetingly looked at me, then her eyes scanned furtively from me to her front door, as if looking for an escape route.

I handed her my card and backed up a step. "Were you home when the police arrived?"

She nodded while looking at my card. I wondered if she was mute until her dog gave me a friendly greeting bark, tail still wagging.

"Elsa, be quiet. Down, girl."

"She's beautiful," I said. "I like the name Elsa."

The woman briefly smiled and extended her hand. "I'm Jane Hadsall. Yes, I was here. The police cars came in with lights and sirens and woke me up."

I prompted her to keep talking. "That was really late."

"Yes, after one."

"Had you seen or heard anything unusual earlier?"

She looked at my card once more, brows knotted, again glancing at her front door. "Who did you say you work for?"

"It's a private investigation related to insurance." Close enough.

Her face cleared. "Oh. Well. No, I don't remember anything strange. I walked Elsa a little after nine. Del and I'd gone out to dinner. It was later than she usually gets walked, and she was whining at the door when we came in. I remember that all the lights in his place were on."

"Was that unusual?"

She thought for a moment. "Yes. I guess so. I don't remember seeing them all on like that before unless he had guests."

"Did he have guests very often?"

Just then a man stuck his head out of her front door. Slicked back dark hair complemented horn-rimmed glasses out of the fifties. He wore a checkered shirt and jeans.

Fear flickered across her face. "Hardly ever. He seemed to be a private person."

The man threw the door open, lumbered up and stood unsteadily between us, reeking of beer and arching his back. "Who're you? Why're you talkin' to m'wife?"

Ms. Hadsall said, "It's all right, Del. He's an insurance investigator looking into our neighbor's death."

"Well, we din' have nuthin' ta do with it. Git the hell off m'propity."

She put her hand on his shoulder. "Now, honey."

He glanced over his shoulder, shrugging off her hand. "Don' 'now honey' me." He clenched his fists at his sides and stepped forward until our chests were almost touching. His breath made my eyes water. "Git outta here."

We were standing on a public sidewalk. I didn't want to fuel the anger I felt rising in me, so I put my hands up, palms out. Backing away, I said to Ms. Hadsall, "Thanks. I'll be in touch if I need anything else," then turned and walked to my car with Del muttering obscenities all the way.

I had intended to talk with other neighbors, too, but I figured Del wouldn't go back indoors until I left, and I didn't feel like being attacked by a jealous drunk.

❧❧ ❧❧ ❧❧

Next morning's Indy Star identified Nicholas by name and mentioned his place of employment in a small article buried in the Metro Section. As soon as I was on the road at a quarter to eight, I
phoned Tito.

"Hi, Wolf. Doing okay?"

"Yeah. The Star had a blurb on Nicholas' death this morning.
Any news on that?"

"There are details that haven't been released to the public."

"Like what?"

"Come on. You know I can't answer that. But you might ask me
a couple of specific questions and I may answer them, especially if
you have information that's related."

"OK. What was the time of death?"

"You have related information?"

"I believe so."

"All right, time of death was seven-thirty, plus or minus an
hour. Now, whatcha got?"

"Still trying to rule out suicide?"

"Could be. Why?"

"Because a neighbor said that every light in the condo was on
when she walked her dog after nine. When I got there, the place
was totally dark."

"So?"

"Think, Tito. If Red committed suicide, how could he turn off
the lights after he was dead?"

Tito was silent for a while. "Well, the only way would be if they
were on a timer. We'll check that out."

"Do that. I'll bet you don't find one, especially one that controls
every light in the condo. That'll rule out suicide, right?"

"Looks like it."

I paused to let that sink in. "You going to start a homicide investigation?"

"I don't make that decision, but, yeah, probably."

Now it was clear that Red Nicholas was murdered. I called Pat Acton and gave him the news. My task for him and Maltrack was complete.

But who had killed him? What was the motive? What did the missing laptop mean?

My bulldog personality wouldn't let go of the case. The meeting with Burberry might shed some light, so I decided to stay on the case on my own dime.

I parked in the underground garage at First Hoosier Tower and rode an elevator that moved so fast my ears popped. I could still hear the background Christmas music, but I didn't feel jolly.

The receptionist buzzed me in and confirmed that I was expected, then directed me to Burberry's office. We settled into chairs at a small conference table with a view of the downtown canal.

"Pat Acton called me yesterday," he said. "Told me about Red's death, and that you might want to see me. I read about it in this morning's paper."

"What the Star didn't say was that his death now appears to be murder. IMPD homicide guys will interview you, but I wonder if you could give me any idea of someone who might have wanted to see him dead. Did he have enemies?"

Burberry smiled thinly. "I've been thinking about that. He and I were fairly close, and since we've both been working in the cybersecurity area, there are a couple of things that might be relevant."

I nodded. "Go ahead."

"His full-time job with Maltrack was what paid the bills. But he was more excited about, you could even say passionate about, computer privacy. He had recently discovered a nasty piece of malware being developed to access personal information by a local ISP."

"How?"

"A Christmas promotion would offer each of their subscribers a discount to extend their contract a year. When they click the attachment to provide payment information, malware is installed on their computer that records every keystroke they make and then downloads them every night."

"So, they would lose account IDs, passwords, credit card info—the works. You think that provided a reason to neutralize him?"

"That's an interesting question. The answer is complicated by his messy divorce that Pat probably told you about."

"How so?"

"His ex-wife—goes by her maiden name Bonnie Walton—works for the ISP as a systems analyst. She's a contractor. Works about half-time from home, half at the office."

"Interesting."

"That's not all. She also stands to benefit financially from his death. The two of them still co-owned the house she's living in. Their divorce settlement about three years ago required that he take out an insurance policy that would pay off the mortgage in case of his death."

"Did he say how much?"

"He said a few months ago they still owed almost two hundred grand on the house."

I thanked Burberry for his time and left without mentioning the missing laptop. Nicholas' ex-wife and the ISP organization each stood to gain by his death.

I was convinced that the laptop would lead to the guilty party or parties. I called Pat Acton as I drove to the offices of the ISP.

When he came on the line, I told him about the Christmas hacking scam.

"I know the ISP," I said. "How soon can you get on this?"

"We can start looking right away, but it's a fishing expedition. The fish has to be swimming where we're fishing."

Stirring up Bonnie Walton was a logical next step. I arrived unannounced at the ISP offices in an office building near Keystone and 86th. I told the receptionist I wanted to see Ms. Walton.

"Why do you wish to speak with her?" she asked.

"Regarding insurance."

"Who do you represent?"

"Wolf Ruger Associates." As I expected, she only glanced at the card I shoved under her nose.

After a brief conversation, the receptionist said, "She's very busy today, but she'll see you here in the lobby for a few minutes."

Ms. Walton blew in like a cyclone, her skinny four-foot-eleven frame sporting a sweatshirt, jeans, and spiked hair. Her too-tapered face was accentuated by a sharp chin and wide eyes. Dark circles under her eyes suggested sleep deprivation.

"Who are you? I'm not interested in buying insurance," she said, never looking me in the eye.

"Wolf Ruger. It's about the homeowner's policy your ex-husband had with us. There seem to be a few expensive items missing from his residence."

"So?"

"We're checking with people who might know where they're located."

"Why me? I haven't seen him for three frickin' years." Her eyes narrowed and flickered briefly, as she turned on her heel, clearly agitated.

"Sorry, Ms. Walton. I'm just interviewing people on the list I was given," I said to her retreating back.

I called Pat from my car. "Any luck with the MAC address trace?"

"No, not yet."

"Keep monitoring. Call me if you get anything."

Back in Broad Ripple, I picked up a bold coffee at Java Joe's, and went upstairs to my office overlooking the corner of Broad Ripple and Guilford. If Maltrack was successful, my hunch was the laptop would be at the ISP's labs.

An hour later, while I was inspecting my Marilyn Monroe calendar, Pat Acton called.

"We've located the laptop. Its location is interesting," he said.

"Great. Where is it, and what's so interesting?" I asked.

He gave me the address. It wasn't the ISP's.

"Someone there is linked via fiber to analysis equipment at the ISP," he said. "The interesting part is that it's Red Nicholas' old address. Pretty sure his ex is living there."

The house was in the Meridian Kessler neighborhood, less than ten minutes from my office in Broad Ripple. I slipped my Smith and Wesson into its holster under my jacket and called Tito.

The address belonged to a small limestone dwelling with green and white metal awnings. The empty front porch and barren lawn contrasted with the festively-decorated porches and lawns of the adjacent bungalows. Whoever lived here wasn't feeling the holiday spirit.

I used the tarnished brass knocker. Bonnie Walton opened the door almost immediately. Barefoot, she had a letter opener in her hand. She'd apparently been opening mail piled on the side table I saw behind her in the hall.

"Get the hell out of here," she sneered, attempting to close the door.

PIs wear sturdy shoes for several reasons, one of which is for keeping doors open. I pushed my way inside. Computer equipment was visible through a door into a room being used as an office. Quickly moving around her, I blocked the door.

She lunged at me with the letter opener. I caught her wrist and pushed her down onto an easy chair, drew my revolver, and waited for Tito.

꞉∼ ꞉∼ ꞉∼

The holiday party at Tito and Carmen Rodriguez's home in Speedway was a gala affair. After gorging myself on Tito's carne asada, and Carmen's Christmas cornbake made from an old family recipe, Tito and I retreated to his study.

"So, how's the Nicholas case coming?" I asked.

"Red's ex-wife confessed to killing him. She's being arraigned on second-degree murder charges tomorrow," Tito answered.

"What was her motive?"

"She says that Red's discovery of the malware she helped develop would destroy her career. And she hated him, anyway."

"Nothing to do with the mortgage insurance?"

"She didn't mention it, but money's always a motivator."

"I'm guessing she was at his place for so long after she shot him because she was trying to destroy every shred of evidence about the malware."

"That's my take on it, too. We recovered a lot of material from her house in addition to Red's laptop. She was reprogramming remote access to the ISP analysis equipment when you saw her at work."

"Had she decrypted any information?"

"Only routine info like credit card statements that had a single encryption layer. She claims she was very close to getting the rest of it, though."

"What are you doing with the laptop and other stuff?"

"IMPD turned it over to the FBI special agent leading the Regional Cybercrime Taskforce. He said to thank you. Stopping her from destroying the evidence means that lots of people will have a greener Christmas."

"Let him know he's welcome," I said with a grin. The Maltrack thumb drive had all the data backed up.

But I didn't mention that.

Carmen Rodriguez's Christmas Cornbake

1 box Jiffy Corn Bread Mix

2 eggs beaten

1 Tablespoon sugar

1.5 sticks butter or margarine

1 cup sour cream

1 16-oz can whole corn (not drained)

1 16-oz can creamed corn

Mix together all ingredients.

Pour into ungreased pan.

Bake at 350 degrees for about an hour, or until toothpick inserted in center comes out dry.

Santa Slayer

By T. C. Winters

y bridesmaid dress screamed, *poor unfortunate Cassandra.* The yellow lace would've looked better on Bo Peep than me, a natural redhead. On the bright side, I loved the pearl-white shoes the bride, my college roommate, had chosen to finish the ensemble. Too bad I resembled a two-day-old corpse wrapped in a gunnysack. I hoped the dearly beloved gathered in Saint John the Evangelist Catholic Church in downtown Indianapolis remembered we were there for wedding vows, not last rights for my dress.

After the ceremony, open carriages—meant to offer a festive ride under the Christmas lights—provided no protection against the biting December wind. We circled the arctic block-by-block, for the sole purpose of viewing the holiday splendor of costumed characters, dancing elves, and decorations, before being saved from frostbite by our epic entrance into the Grand Hall at historic Union Station for the reception. While impressed with the grandeur of the stately marble floors, original woodwork, and stained glass, I positioned myself on the backside of the massive bar, drinking ginger ale. Given my foul mood, refraining from socializing was a public service.

About two hours into the celebration, the best man sidled up beside me, his gaze never leaving my boobs as he sloshed red wine on my hideous three-hundred-dollar dress—the third bridesmaid dress

I'd been forced to wear this year. My popularity as an attendant was due less to friendship and more to pity because last year, my own December wedding had ended with the groom taking a pass.

Frowning, I dabbed at the stain spreading across my bodice as the bride rushed to my side, her white-blonde hair escaping from the elegant updo.

Grabbing a bar towel, she pressed it against the bright red blotch blooming over my chest. "Cassandra, you poor thing. December hasn't been a good month for you, has it?"

The question was rhetorical, and I only grunted my reply.

The bride patted my arm as she left, and my desire to evaporate into thin air intensified.

A bozo duo sauntered beside me, one short, one tall. The tall one lurched forward, smelling of whiskey and sweat. Using his glass to punctuate, he said, "If I told you that you had a beautiful body would you hold it against me?"

Not charmed, I slid my ginger ale farther down the bar and repositioned myself. In unison, they moved closer, the smaller one attached to the hip of the taller one as if a ventriloquist dummy. The dummy surprised me by speaking.

"You're over here by yourself acting like you're too good for the rest of us because you're some big shot investigative reporter on TV." His hand flashed forward and caught my nipple through the stained yellow lace, twisting until pain burst.

I jacked his male bits with the pointy tip of my pearl-white shoe.

He went down hard, screaming and grabbing his crotch.

With a roar, his companion lunged, swaying off balance, but the best man intercepted him. Two groomsmen swept in, followed by friends of the two clowns. The alcohol fueled fight that ensued was YouTube worthy.

I thought everything had been handled, but the cops showed

up anyway. I didn't do cops—at least not anymore. Darting for my coat, I sprinted across the gleaming marble floors and exited through the heavy brass doors onto the sidewalk. Making a right at the Omni Severin Hotel on Jackson Place, I headed for the Ike and Jonesy's iconic Marilyn Monroe sign, my mouth watering at the scent of fried foods. The narrow lane, awash with the joys of Christmas, was nearly deserted except for Santa Claus ringing a brass bell over a kettle. Having spent a minimal amount of money at the cash bar, I approached and opened my evening bag, dumping the change into the red bucket. Before he uttered a word, the rat-a-tat-tat of what I thought was a snare drum bounced off the surrounding buildings.

Santa melted into a red velvet heap—a black hole adorning his forehead.

I froze, but a sound similar to that of a congested cat drew my attention toward McCrea Street where a bulky outline transformed into a man—overweight, hunched over, and limping. He huffed and glanced over his shoulder in my direction before disappearing into the pall of a poorly lit parking lot.

My mouth opened but no sound escaped. As I fought the urge to vomit, a woman exiting Ike and Jonesy's nightclub screamed, returning my attention to Dead Santa. The woman back-peddled and disappeared into the quirky nightclub, leaving me to stare at my blood-spattered pearl-white shoes. Unable to process, I froze, even as the hammer of footsteps running on the sidewalk grew closer.

A two-hundred-pound Rudolph plowed into me, sandwiching my body to the icy concrete, grinding my face into the salty Icy Melt, and cracking at least one rib. Pain seared and warm blood trailed down my neck. Not from a hole in my head, but from my lip kissing the stony sidewalk.

Rudolph's head flew off, revealing none other than my cold-footed former fiancé; only there was nothing cold about him.

"What the…?" I eyed the gun angled above my head as every muscle in his body met mine like a memory foam mattress.

He slapped a large paw over my face, forcing my head down. "Stop struggling."

I clamped down on the fear and concentrated on my hatred stemming from the humiliation he'd caused almost one year ago. "Get off of me, you filthy caribou." I rolled to one side, trying to dislodge him, but ended up on my back with his big body between my legs. His fur smelled of knock-you-on-your-ass-BO, and I averted my head to keep from gagging.

He rewarded my efforts by leaping upward and dragging my limp body across the sidewalk. Once safely behind the brick wall of a neighboring building, he patted at the wine and blood stains on my dress. "Blood. Where were you hit?"

"Not…no…just my lip…wine stain…his blood." I glanced at the abandoned Rudolph head lying near the dead Santa. "If this is some kind of an elaborate hoax to get my attention, you can peddle your reindeer games somewhere else, buddy."

Detective Mac Muldoon had once been all I'd wanted for Christmas. Mac was my polar opposite, with his dark hair and eyes a wicked shade of blue. We would have made beautiful babies. We'd met when I was assigned to the crime beat for the local news station. My boss believed tossing a greenhorn investigative reporter into the rancid cesspool thriving in the city's underbelly was a just reward for being forced to hire me because my on-air presence boosted ratings. Not only had the viewers embraced my fair-skinned Irish appearance, so had the members of the Indianapolis Metro Police Department.

All thoughts of a hoax evaporated as SWAT swarmed the alley, securing the area. Mac pulled me to my feet, and under cover of a riot shield, hustled me to the east side of Union Station where the downtown district of IMPD was located. Shedding his reindeer costume and the Kevlar hidden underneath, Mac morphed from woodland critter to calm professional. Hauling me along, he barked orders to the uniformed officers who huddled around folding tables overflowing with maps.

The downtown branch of IMPD consisted primarily of the bike and horse patrol officers, most of whom dealt with drunk and disorderly conduct and an occasional shooting, so the amount of activity surprised me. Curiosity was one of my fatal flaws, and I craned my neck to see what had absorbed their attention, but Mac found an empty office and nudged me inside.

"How badly are you hurt?" His tone would have been no less harsh if he'd asked where I'd hidden the body.

Instinctively, I pressed a hand to my ribs and took an exploratory inhale. Fishing hooks grappled in my lungs, but I exhaled slowly and met his gaze. "I'm fine. Looks like a command center has been set up. What's happening? Why are you dressed like Rudolph?"

In answer, he marched toward me and manhandled my ribcage with a probing finger. "Did you see the shooter?"

I flinched and batted at his hand. "Not very well. The shot came from behind me, and when I turned, he popped out of the shadows." I stepped away from the funky fusion of masculine and caribou scent.

"You saw the shooter and you're injured." Using his six-feet-four height as leverage, he frowned down at me. "You're going to the hospital under a protective detail." His hostile stare was no doubt meant to reduce me to a blubbering mass.

I had an urge to spit in his face, but I'd just had the spit scared out of me, leaving me unable to perform. My annoyance ratcheted and my mouth was in motion before my brain reacted. "Obviously with someone other than you since your idea of protection was pulling out early."

With a remarkably gentle touch, he redirected me to the main concourse. "Sawyer, take Miss Flynn to the emergency room. No lights, but don't leave her side."

Sawyer, a skinny guy who looked about twelve, nodded, and with a sweep of his arm indicated I should follow. When we were out of earshot from Mac, he said, "Hey, you're that news lady. My mom watches you every night."

I smiled as my youth gave me the finger from the ledge on which it was precariously perched. "Please tell her I appreciate the loyalty." My mind hamster-wheeled as I followed him to his squad car. Waiting until we were strapped in and the car was in motion, I said, "Sure was hopping in there tonight. Any luck with the investigation?" I snuck a sideways glance at him to see if he'd taken the bait.

My bluff worked because he sat up straighter and lowered the squawking from his radio. "Your guy was the third Santa hit today. The others were within minutes apart earlier this evening, and we still don't have a motive. Union Station was central to the shootings, so that's where we set up command."

The information took a second to absorb into my still-shocked brain. "Why haven't the Santas been told to stay off the streets?"

"We've tried to get the word out, but it's not like there's a union we can contact. Some of the Santas aren't with the Salvation Army, they're community volunteers, so detectives dressed in costumes are walking the streets to warn and protect them."

"Any leads on the identity of the Santa Slayer?" As a member of the media, I couldn't help but coin a cutesy phrase that would play well on air.

Sawyer chuckled but didn't take his eyes off the road. "Santa Slayer. I like that." He darted a quick peek in my direction. "The first Santa was some bigwig at PNC bank. The second was a self-employed CPA. We're looking for a connection but so far nothing. Your guy didn't have ID on him."

Despite Mac's request to not use the lights, Sawyer had flipped his on during the heavy weekend night traffic, and we arrived at IU Health Hospital in less than ten minutes. Because of my police escort, I was assigned a room before the ink on my signature dried, but the Saturday night crowd had been howling at more than the moon, and the place was rocking.

The ER visit went relatively fast, considering. With my cracked rib shrink-wrapped, and my ruined dress bagged for evidence, the only advice the doc gave me was to rest and take Advil for the next six weeks. While I exchanged the hospital gown, open in back to provide maximum humiliation, for a pair of scrubs, bells jingled from the hallway. I pulled the curtain to find a gorgeous man dressed in Santa pants and an unbuttoned Santa coat prowling the hallway in front of my cubicle, a white beard dangling from his fingertips. My fatal flaw convinced me to investigate, and I slipped out. Half-dressed Santa, looking like a cover model, stopped in front of a cubicle a few curtains past mine, wringing the beard like worry beads. Tugging the hem of the scrubs, I stepped around the carnage common to all ERs and snuck up beside him as he paced between three side-by-side cubicles.

The smell emanating from the rooms was that of an unattended litter box. Inside all three areas was a scene straight out of Misery The Musical. Three Santas, sans beards and topcoats, were puking into kidney shaped bowls while nurses stood off to the side, holding damp cloths.

I edged up to the only Santa left standing. "What happened?"

"Food poisoning. Probably the eggnog."

A young woman in scrubs bustled by, speaking as she whisked into the middle stall. "Not food poisoning. The urine analysis shows high levels of arsenic. These men were poisoned."

My Santa, since in the few seconds I'd laid eyes on him I'd come to think of him as mine, dropped his beard and inhaled so sharply

I considered giving him the Heimlich. "Wh…what? We were at a party." His face held a quizzical expression. "I don't drink."

Doesn't drink? A sure reject on my dating profile.

The lure of a good story helped me recover from my shattered dream. "Was anyone else dressed as the jolly old elf?"

Confusion shone in his eyes, and he offered a half-hearted shrug. "No, just the four of us. We were supposed to be working after hours collecting money near Circle Centre Mall for a special project, but the cops made us leave. We went to the party instead."

I moved in for the kill. "What party?"

"The Capital Improvements Board's holiday party." He made a whirling motion with his finger that encompassed himself and his three hapless buddies. "We're on the board."

Sawyer, who'd been sitting at the opposite end of the hall, wormed his way past the ER personnel and came to a stop beside me, resting his hand on my shoulder. "We need to go back. Detective Muldoon wants your statement."

Divesting myself of his hand by rolling my shoulder, I whispered to Only-Santa-Left- Standing, "Was a large man with a limp at the party?"

He tilted his head and ran a hand through his fabulous mahogany mane. "Yeah, there was a guy with a limp. Older, plump, wearing a dark sweatshirt and dark pants. I remember because I didn't know him and he looked out of place. I thought he might've been a party crasher, looking for free booze."

Sawyer parked his hand on my shoulder again, this time applying enough pressure to force my attention. "Detective Muldoon needs you."

"He only *thinks* he needs me. He'll recant soon enough."

Expelling a heavy sigh, he propelled me toward the main door, stopping so I could sign release papers.

Sawyer must have been worried about Mac's legendary black

temper because he blasted the siren and lights all the way back to the downtown district headquarters. Instead of parking the car, he dumped me near the front entrance, but he did escort me to the door.

Inside, the chaos had amped-up. More people filled the space and everyone seemed to be in a flurry of motion. Mac Muldoon stood front and center in the mayhem, gesturing wildly and shouting orders.

Charging like a hungry panther when he noticed me, he hooked my arm and weaved through the throng until we came to a vacant conference room. Closing the door, he said, "We need to talk."

"Damn straight we do. Why'd you dump me?" I'd been so pissed at his defection that I'd refused to take his calls.

"Being with you was like always being on air. We had no privacy. *I* had no privacy." Flopping into a chair, he propped his elbows onto the table. "That's not what I meant when I said we needed to talk. You saw the assailant, and he saw you. You're well known in this community, so he could've recognized you."

He had a point on both counts. I'd been so captivated with Mac and my vision of our future together, that his betrayal had decimated my spirit. I'd been busy molding my career and hadn't given any consideration to how the constant circuit of business dinners had affected my reserved betrothed. I loved to hate him because doing so usurped my own sense of culpability, but now wasn't the time to pick at the festered scab over my jilted heart. Another year older and another year wiser, I understood the error of my ways. And I *had* seen the shooter, someone who at this point could be considered a spree killer.

I stood between Mac and the door. Weighing my options, I did a one-eighty and pushed open the door.

He caught me by the wrist. "Don't leave. I'm sorry for being an ass, but I died a thousand deaths when I saw you standing near that slain Santa. I thought you were next." He eased me into a chair. "I need a description, then we'll assign you a security detail until the shooter's caught."

Relenting, I gave him a description of the man, including On-ly-Santa-Left-Standing's description of his clothing, but I didn't add how I'd obtained that particular element. I planned to discover if the dead Santas were on the Capital Improvements Board, then research who'd have a motive to kill them. "I don't need some rookie who's been banished to babysitting detail dogging my every step."

"I'm not assigning a rookie. I'm going to cover you myself." He blinked hard, as if he'd realized the double meaning.

With a dramatic sniff, I rose. "As much as I've missed being *covered* by you, I've discovered I'm quite proficient in…covering myself."

Nary a muscle moved on his face, but he narrowed his eyes. "No need. I found that aspect of our relationship to be quite sat-isfactory."

My hackles raised, upped the ante, and called. "Satisfactory?" I'd thought that "aspect" had been bombs-bursting-in-air fabulous.

He raised his eyebrows into a critical arch. "Maybe my memo-ry's faulty. If you'd like a do-over—"

This time I stormed out of the room, past the command center, and out the front doors. Barely two steps outside, a truck backfired, and I hit the sidewalk.

Mac reached down. "My house or yours?" He pulled me up and dusted off my scrubs.

"Mine. I need my computer for research." Admitting I was wrong had never been one of my finer traits.

⁓ ⁓ ⁓

Mac toddling around my house in the wee hours of the morning severely cramped my style. With my laptop open on my bed, I slammed the lid every time footsteps neared my bedroom door. Before our breakup—something the primitive part of my brain acknowledged might have been my fault—Mac had suffered from insomnia, so his rambling brought back memories.

In between his roaming footsteps, I'd pulled up IndyStar.com and searched for information on the slain Santas, then cross-referenced their names with the Capital Improvements Board website. Both were on the CIB managers list. No mention had been made in the news of the sick Santas in the ER, but Only-Santa-Left-Standing had said they were on the CIB, so I pulled up their glamour shots and *voila*—names, and occupations. Several more taps on the keyboard and I culled an article with a photo about the CIB board members, along with other organizations, dressing as Santa to collect money for charity. All nine of the current board members stared back at me as if red velvet was in vogue.

Once Mac's solitary footfalls quieted, I began the arduous task of searching for a link between the CIB managers and a disgruntled constituent. The board had been granted the right of eminent domain, and in the past decade, multiple stories of unhappy property owners had circulated in the press.

After several mind-numbing hours of searching, I located an article on the death of a woman whose husband had been a well-respected local businessman named Chester Rogers. A blurry video of the funeral showed her husband, a middle-aged, overweight, Caucasian with a limp, walking beside her casket. The story went on to detail how she'd committed suicide after her hubby had refused to sell a property to the CIB. He accused the board of retaliating by tattling to the local police about the building's use as a swinger's club. For several weeks after the wife's death, the media had dogged the man's every step, exposing not only an illicit affair, but also a child born out of wedlock. Months later, he'd filed for bankruptcy and lost his business. The CIB got his property, and he got the shaft.

While searching for a phone number for Chester Rogers, I speculated on why I hadn't made the connection sooner. The press had slobbered over the story for weeks, but I'd been working on a feature story that would subsequently launch my career and hadn't been paying attention. Finding Roger's cell number, I sent a text.

Mac burst into my room, his laptop cradled against his chest. "What haven't you told me?" Dismissing my attempt at a faux astonished expression, he said, "When you were so quiet I knew you were up to something. You haven't changed your Wi-Fi and iCloud passwords since I left. You've been obstructing justice from the comfort of your bed."

"You can't use my passwords without my permission."

He held the computer aloft. "I just did."

"That pesky fourth amendment. I'm assuming your interpretation of unreasonable search doesn't include *my* private information."

His expression indicated civil rights weren't his top priority. "Apparently you've made a connection with the CIB and our slain Santas."

The look he shot my way threatened a pox on my future lineage, but I was a seasoned professional. I rolled my shoulders and elevated my brows to bite-me stage.

"This," he speared the air above my head with his finger, "*this* is what I mean about placing your career before anything else."

Relenting, I laid out everything I'd found and finished with, "He chose to kill them while they were dressed as Santa to make a statement. Knowing I can identify him might make him contact me in the hopes the media attention will help him gain public sympathy."

"Or he'll kill you."

"Maybe so, but he isn't finished." I handed Mac a sticky note that included three former CIB managers. "Here's the other three names on his hit list. They aren't currently on the board, so they aren't doing the Santa thing, but they were on the board during this incident." What I didn't hand my ex Mr. Right was my phone, the new one not yet hooked up to my Wi-Fi. On it was the time and place Chester Rogers, the likely Santa Slayer, had agreed to meet.

Mac snatched the paper. "If you'd told me earlier we could've put these people in protective custody."

Turning the computer screen, I showed him a list of the sick Santas. "These guys, too. They were poisoned and are probably still at the hospital." I pointed to Last-Santa-Left-Standing. "Except for him. He wasn't on the board then." I willed Mac to hurry up because I was meeting Mr. Rogers at a playground in under an hour.

Mac fished his phone from his pocket. Jabbing numbers on the screen, he bellowed orders to the poor soul on the other end. Two more quick calls and he addressed me. "A new security detail is five minutes out. Stay inside with the doors locked until they get here." His face darkened and another hex on my future offspring winged my way.

"When have I not listened to you?"

Mac ignored my comment, or maybe he grunted, I wasn't sure, but once he left and his headlights faded from my driveway, I called my cameraman who said I was an idiot. I agreed, then changed clothes, Googled the address in my phone message, and went off to slay dragons.

Indianapolis contained a patchwork of ethnic neighborhoods, and my route took me through enough nationalities to form the United Nations. The sun had not yet peeked through the brightening sky, and the roads were nearly deserted. I reached the playgrounds in Ellenberger Park on the far eastside with fifteen minutes to spare.

I parked the car and walked toward the playground where the empty equipment stood in deep shadows. A light breeze set the swings in motion, the sudden movement nearly seizing my lungs. I dug my pepper spray from my purse and clamped it in my palm, listening for approaching footsteps, hearing nothing but the pounding of my heart. Allowing my eyes to adjust to the low light of the sunrise, I stumbled through the crunchy sand, shook the snow off the rubbery swing seat, and gripped the chains. Before I could settle, a hand clamped over my mouth. I never had a chance to deploy the pepper spray before it was lights out.

I woke up duct taped to the swing. With my brains scrambled, my sense of time was distorted. Shaking off the cobwebs, I took in my surroundings, but my spinal cord seemed fused and my range of motion was limited. My hands were bound, but I was able to raise them high enough to touch my neck, where something scratchy and cold abraded my skin. Feeling with my fingers, I encountered a wire looped around my neck, like a noose. Attached to the end of the loop was a sawed-off shotgun, pointed straight at my skull.

"I've wired the trigger to my index finger. If anything happens to me, even an accidental trip, kaboom. Your brains get splattered," said a shrill voice I assumed belonged to Chester Rogers.

I twisted my body, carefully drawing the contraption along with my movements, and faced the man who held me captive.

Murky blue eyes, the color of water churning in an angry ocean, never stopped moving. "You're the doll on the local news, right?"

Too afraid to move further, I lifted my chin a fraction of an inch in response.

"I got the idea after you messaged me. Cops is on their way. So's your TV station. When I called they said they was already headed here." He nudged me with his free hand. "Couldn't resist a good story, huh?"

He continued speaking in a high-pitched voice, but I tuned out the madman's ranting in favor of focusing on the distant sirens that grew louder with each shaky breath.

Mac was right. I'd made myself a liability because I'd only considered what the story would do for my career. Even if I avoided execution in front of a TV audience, Mac would kill me the first chance he had.

A car door slammed, then chunks of frozen sand sprayed close to my shoes as Mac screeched to a halt within a few feet of my position. One quick visual revolution around my throat, and his face blanched. He turned his attention to the Santa Slayer. "Tony Kiritsis, 1977. Interesting choice to emulate. What's Miss Flynn done to earn your wrath?"

Gesturing with his left hand, Rogers said, "Déjà vu Indy style. Kiritsis got his say in front of the cameras. She's the golden ticket to mine."

Mac backed away, his palm held out in front. "Cassandra, he has a shotgun wired in a dead-man's switch so no one can shoot him. Any movement and the gun goes off. Do you understand?"

Paralyzed with fear, I said, "Yes." My voice sounded like a yelp.

"Chester, the news crew is right behind me. If I let them move forward, do you promise you'll not pull the trigger?"

Chester shifted his feet.

The noose tightened.

"Bring 'em in."

Blake, my cameraman for the past two years, scuttled forward until he stood in front of me. He hoisted the camera to his shoulder, but his terrified gaze never left my face. "We're rolling."

Rogers yanked the wire around my neck in an apparent attempt to heighten the drama. "I'm here to report the unfair acts inflicted by the CIB. We live in the damned United States, but the damned government can still steal a man's damn property."

He droned on and with every curse-filled sentence he became

more unhinged. Crews from competing stations began lining the fence surrounding the playground, each wanting their shot at a juicy story. Fragments of excited conversation floated, but Mac never moved, not even to blink.

I kept my gaze on his face until the dripping sweat stung my eyes. My head grew heavy and I dropped my chin to my chest. Time slowed as Rogers running monologue of profanity and hatred became more heated. A sharp tug forced my head up.

I cringed, anticipating the burning pain of a bullet.

I opened my eyes. Mac's lips moved, but no sound came as he advanced toward us, his hands up in a submissive position, and his steps slow and measured. Apparently, Rogers had finished whatever he wanted to say, because Mac freed Rogers' finger from the trigger, then wiggled the gun away from my neck.

Officers charged, duty belts crackling, and shoes whispering across the sand, before they slammed Rogers to the ground.

Mac handed off the shotgun and lifted me away from the swing. My legs wouldn't support my weight, and I stumbled. He wheeled me into his arms and carried me toward an ambulance waiting near the pulsating throng of news crews. As we passed, they called out, begging for a highlight.

"*What was your role with the Santa Slayer?*"

"*How long were you held hostage?*"

"*Cassandra! Over here, Cassandra!*"

Being in Mac's arms again was more satisfying than a ratings hike.

I buried my face in the crook of his neck and turned my back on the cameras.

Santa's Eggnog

3 eggs, slightly beaten

1/2 cup granulated sugar

2 1/2 cups whole milk

1 teaspoon plus 1/2 teaspoon vanilla extract

1 cup heavy whipping cream

2 tablespoons powdered sugar

1/2 cup light rum (or for non-alcohol version, 2 tablespoons rum extract mixed with 1/3 cup milk)

Ground nutmeg for garnish

In 2-quart heavy saucepan, stir eggs and granulated sugar until well mixed. Gradually stir in milk. Cook over medium heat 10 to 15 minutes, stirring constantly, until mixture thickens slightly. Remove from heat. Stir in 1 teaspoon vanilla. Let cool, then cover and refrigerate at least 2 hours. Overnight is acceptable.

Just before serving, beat heavy whipping cream, powdered sugar and 1/2 teaspoon vanilla with electric mixer on high speed until stiff peaks form. Gently stir 1 cup of the whipped cream, the rum, and food color into custard.

Pour custard mixture into small punch bowl. Drop remaining whipped cream in mounds onto custard mixture. Sprinkle with nutmeg. Serve immediately. Store in refrigerator up to 2 days.

Makes 10 half-cup servings

Qraven

By B. K. Hart

December 22, 2073 18:36

Death's varied bouquet, familiar places in time, reaching through one's memory. The very long dead…old, dank, mothball farts. The not-so-long dead, partially still in the throes of decay. Its carcass rotting away. A high stench garbage, slightly sweet like vomit. And, the fresh dead and bloody, with high metallic discharges. A clean, almost culinary butchered scent unless bodily fluids were included, in which case, not so culinary.

This guy had a clean, nearly antiseptic odor with a green, squashed, frog-from-the-pond smell.

Crouched next to the corpse, Denver McNulty III used a pen tip and eased the shoulder back so he could get a look at the front side of the victim. A small military tattoo imprint on the neck just below the left ear. Denver felt the presence of watchers, eyes in the shadows, some of them human.

"I know damn well you are not screwing with my crime scene."

Denver slid his gaze toward the wide-open mouth of the re-purposed warehouse, now storage unit. The cobblestone alley disappearing in the darkness behind her backlit form. It was always dark in the undercity. SkyIndy tended to block all natural sunlight to the ground, with the exception of old Military Park where they still let the sunshine through, and some of the rural garden and farm lots. The undercity streets were shiny, wet. Topside still snowed, Thanksgiving through Easter. Undercity held in too much heat, melting any flakes that made it past the upper city limits.

"Lieutenant," he acknowledged.

Aurora Elliott, long-legged, high-heeled, short-skirted in black, silver-sequined on top, long straight silver wig. Holiday lights flashed, green then red, reflecting off her glittery top and shimmering hair.

"Undercover tonight?" he asked.

"Day off," she said with a sulk. The tip flared red as she sucked her cigarette, then she turned and flicked it into the cluttered alleyway behind her. "Where the hell's my forensics? And why are you here?"

"It was on the way home. This *is* my neighborhood."

He allowed himself an appreciative and leisurely perusal of her bare, fit legs. It had been a long time since he'd last seen that much of her thighs.

"See anything interesting?" she said with a smirk. She walked over to stand near the victim's head, squatted and dropped a knee to the concrete floor, flashing a swatch of pink panty.

He wanted to say, nothing he hadn't seen before. But, he'd always found her quite interesting and didn't want to offend. One never knew, did one?

"How much longer is this shit going to take?" Another woman's voice. Becca or Becky, Denver couldn't remember for sure.

"When did you say you bought this unit?" he inquired.

"Three days ago. You know how the auction paperwork goes. You place your bid. They take your money then spend the next two days determining whether you are good enough to buy the crap some loser left behind."

"You discovered the body?" Aurora stood.

"Yeah, City Services finally cleared the unit at the last damn

minute today. I barely had time to set up a light crew to get in here."
She tapped her watch. "They're supposed to be here by seven, and
they ain't cheap. I need to unload this shit within 24 hours or City
Services starts charging me for the unit."

"You're not unloading anything over my dead body," Aurora
said.

"She means, that dead body," Denver qualified, pointing at the
corpse.

"Jesus, he's already attracting rats," Becca said. "Looks like they
started working on his eyes. That's disgusting."

She didn't move away though. In fact, she moved a little closer.

"You know this guy?" Aurora asked.

"No, I told him already. I opened up the storage unit. Saw the
stiff and had to walk halfway up the block to find a red phone that
worked."

Denver was looking at the rat-gnawed eye socket. Only the
wound looked too precise to be the results of a rodent buffet. Using his penlight, he scanned the immediate area coming to rest on a
concave piece of transparent, barely green glass.

"He wasn't killed here," he stated.

Denver reached into his jacket pocket and pulled out an evidence bag and a glove, then he carefully picked up the piece of glass
and put it inside. He held it out for Aurora who took it and held it
up as if there were some other light she could see better by. "This is
just a dumping ground. Not enough blood for one thing. And they
appear to have dumped all his things with him."

"It's a Qraven?" Aurora asked.

"Looks that way," Denver stood, knees popping as he rose. "That
glass looks to be about what you might find around the eye socket."

"You think?" she said shaking the bag then flipping it over to
get a different angle.

Becca said, "Shit always gets real around Christmas time. Sky-

Indy sends down harvesters. Walking around with a Qraven is practically an advertisement to come get your shit."

Denver studied Becca. She said shit a lot. She didn't seem nervous, not really. Agitated, more like.

He was aware of the fad. Like skin stretching, tattoos, piercings. Qraven was the youth of today's rebellion, removing a section of their skin, sometimes bone, so you could see the organs behind it. Eyes weren't uncommon. He'd seen parts of a jaw, exposing the teeth inside. Over the ribs, or ribs removed, exposing the liver or the heart, the kidneys. He didn't understand it. What were the kids thinking, leaving a window to their interiors like that? But, there you were. Qraven. The latest and greatest way for the new generation to tell their parents to screw off.

"I just take out the trash around here, but it looks to me like you need some extra bags," called a new voice.

He was a big guy. Big nose, big hands.

Denver eyed the man warily. "Moose, what brings you to our humble crime scene?"

Every time the trash department was involved with City Services, they had to double check the invoicing. The more you tried to take the trash out of the mob, the more the mob seemed to take out the trash. Denver could think of no good reason for Moose to be on hand.

"I was following these bozos," Moose said pointing over his shoulder. The crime scene techs appeared toting field kits. Along with the techs were the light crew. "Looked like the party was this way. My cousin, Joey, just started with the team, and I thought he might be with 'em. I guess not though, huh?"

"Fall off of your cloud, Mr. Connors?" Aurora asked with an outstretched hand. "We don't see much of your department down here. At least, not anyone above supervisor level."

"You got to watch the little people all the time," Moose said shaking Aurora's hand. He fired up a cigar and proceeded to stink up the small space, even with the big bay door open.

Aurora turned to her crew and began barking out instructions.

One of the new techs came over to the body and took out a piece of chalk. "Whoa, buddy, what are you doing?" Denver asked, raising his hand to halt him.

"I'm just…the outline…"

Aurora spun, took in the new guy with the chalk, and glared at her tech team. "I don't want any of this bullshit happening on my watch, clear?"

Tough to be the new kid.

"Sorry, Lieutenant, it was a joke." Her supervisor dropped his eyes and whispered to the new kid, "Put that away, and get some pictures with the digital camera. You remember angles, right?"

"Scan this guy and tell us who we got," Denver said.

And, they did.

"Dead guy's name is Jason Rice. Works for the trash department."

Every head turned to look at Moose.

⌁ ⌁ ⌁

December 23, 2073 02:35

Denver's apartment was on the seventh floor of a gold-glass converted office building, located three blocks from the storage site where the body had been found. Nine blocks from City Services, where the station house was located, near the old glass and steel bus station which had been built around the turn of the century. Downtown Indianapolis, once a thriving metropolis, was now the seedy underbelly of SkyIndy. Denver, like most city police officers, lived in the center of his district where he could walk, bike, or hoof. The county and state departments had vehicles, but most of the municipalities relied on good old pedestrian transportation. Districts were small. He worked the old mall region, from the station house west across Washington Street to the government center dump yard, and up to just inside of the north/south I65 split.

Exhausted, he tossed his keys in the catchall next to the front door and closed his eyes for a moment.

"Rough night?"

He turned. Clad in a pair of bikini briefs and nothing else, Kati was eating from a container that looked suspiciously like his leftover Chinese from last night.

"Put some clothes on."

She huffed, slammed the oyster pail down on the table and put her hands on her hips. "You know its people like you, with your outdated, prudish ideas of the human body who continue to sexualize women and make our society a cesspool of depravity for rapists and abusers."

Teens.

"Kati, can we not do this today?"

"What would be a good day, Denver? Should I have you pencil me in?"

"I'm beat. I had a long night. And, you know you can live with your mother if you don't like my uptight rules about putting clothes on in the house. Call me old-fashioned. If you were still a toddler, it would be a different story. As an adult, I am asking you to put some damn clothes on."

"Why should I?"

"Because I'm your father, and I said so!"

She gave him the squinty eye, shook her head, and stormed off in the direction of her bedroom. "You could say thank you for the Christmas tree."

He fingered a branch on the pitiful looking stubby pine. She had wrapped a thin gauzy gold ribbon in a spiral around the sparse needles. Crystals hung from a few of the branches. Denver appreciated the effort.

He went to the kitchen, grabbed a beer out of the fridge and went back to the dining table. He sat, swigged half of the beer and picked up the chopsticks. It was his damn leftovers after all. He took a bite of the cold Moo Shu Pork. Kati had left papers scattered across the table. She had obviously been in the middle of something before he interrupted her.

Lease Your Body Marketing
Rent your Forehead for $5000
The body billboard, how you too can make
$50,000 by leasing your...

"Hey," he yelled. "What the hell is this stuff on the table?"

He heard her grumbling but couldn't make out the words. He flipped through a catalogue on tattooing, and then one on Qraven art. What was she thinking? All he could see was the dead guy in the alley missing his glass piece, along with the eyeball that used to be behind it.

"Get your half-clad fanny back in here!"

"Coming!" She half skipped, half ran back then slid into a chair across from him, t-shirt hanging just barely past the crotch line of her panties. She frowned at his chopsticks. "Hey, I was eating that."

He pushed the container over to her. One finger tapped the high-gloss brochures.

"Talk to me."

"I was looking at skin art. There's nothing to it." She shrugged.

"You know how dangerous this Qraven stuff is right now?" He opened the pages to a head shot and pushed it across the table at her. "My case tonight was a guy with this one right here."

"And?" she sulked.

"And they killed him for his eye."

"That's like urban legend, Dad."

He slapped his hand against the table, the updraft causing some of the pages to scoot across the surface. Kati jumped in her chair. "Try to pretend I know a little from my job. It's not a myth. Kids are losing their lives to this stuff."

"Look," she hesitated. "It might have been true at one time but this guy," she pointed to the one with the socket exposed, "you wouldn't kill this guy for his eye for two reasons. One, he'd sell it to you, very likely replacing it with a glass eye. It's still a novelty, and that's the point. Two, he has two eyes so you don't just take one, you take both, and losing your eyes doesn't kill you. It just leaves you blind. It makes no sense."

Denver leaned back in his chair and stared at his daughter. She was right. He had been looking at the obvious. All of them had been looking at the obvious. He needed to run through some additional search criteria when he returned to the office. He needed some serious sleep first. He was wiped out. Denver ran a hand across his face. He was missing connections.

"So, you aren't planning to have this done?" he asked.

Kati jumped up and disappeared into the kitchen. "Want another beer?"

"No. I need a bed. Are you not answering my question?"

"I am answering. Beer doesn't go well with cookies anyway," she said, and she slid back into a chair a bit closer to him this time. She set a plate of gingerbread cookies in front of him, then handed him a martini glass of Christmas cheer. She gave him a sly look, sliding her eyes over the pamphlets. "I knew you'd hate those if you saw them."

She slid another glossy pamphlet toward him. He took a sip of the cinnamon enhanced martini. "So you resort to bribery? Liquor me up, fill me with sugar. Figure to soften me up then spring the degeneracy you really wanted?"

"Is it working?"

"What is it you want, a piercing?"

"No, it's light."

He looked at the cover. A man with florescent stripes from cheekbone to forehead. A box section with a woman's hand, the back of each finger lit up with a rainbow of color...pinky in red, thumb in purple. He opened the booklet to another full page of pictures, each showing skin that glowed with a multitude of patterns.

"What is this?"

"It's bioluminescence. It's leading edge technology using plant and animal life, natural fluorescence. Like what they have been working on with street lighting. Only now you can program certain cells to mimic the technology."

"So you want your body parts lighting up?"

"I was actually thinking about my hair!" Kati cried. "I haven't seen it on hair, and Danita says the real problem is the hair grows so fast, as soon as you get it glowing, it's going to fade away an inch every few weeks. Whereas there is a CRISPR technique which has been used for editing genomes in plants which can adhere plant to human DNA and alter the actual hair follicle. That's kind of a lame explanation, it's actually more like an RNA transplant, but I am getting way over your head."

Denver held up his hand. "Find me more information to read. I'll talk to Danita. And, let me get some sleep so I can have a rational conversation about it? I suppose you wanted this for your Christmas present. I'm not saying yes..."

She squealed and wrapped her arms around his neck. "You're the best! I don't care what Mom says."

᠅   ᠅   ᠅

December 23, 2073 10:13

The rhythmic thud of the tennis ball, as it bounced off the wall, helped him think. Denver spent a restless night mentally reviewing the crime scene, the conversations, trying to put his finger on what felt off. It was Kati's comment more than anything. *You don't kill a guy for his eyes.* His chair was twisted to the side so he could prop his feet on the gray desktop and still hit the wall.

She doesn't care what her mom says. Did he actually let her get away with that? *Man, I must have been tired.*

He tossed the ball again. Thump. Thump. Thump.

"Yo, McNulty."

"Yeah, Carmichael, what do you want? I'm trying to think here."

"Yeah? Think about this." Carmichael grabbed his pants by the crotch and yanked it twice.

"I'm going for expanded consciousness, Carmichael, not preponderance of the small and insignificant."

There were a few low-key snickers from the squad room.

"You think you're funny? You're 'bout as funny as a pimple on a comedian's butt. You want this transmission code on your stiff or not?"

"You got a code on my stiffy?"

More snickers. One loud guffaw.

"Smart guy." He threw the code down on Denver's desk with a frown and waddled away.

Denver hid a grin, dropped his feet to the floor and squared off with his desk. He pulled up a transmission screen and accessed the report. He brushed a finger across the text and found the first page and began to read. Nothing significant. Address. DOB. Current position. Credit score and history. Interesting, since he didn't show up "on paper" until seven years ago. That sent a small worm into his brain. Why would a guy not show credits until seven years ago? In fact, remembering one small detail from the body, Denver knew this was impossible.

A secondary file was attached to the report in video format. He opened it and scanned through the video and the still-shots of the crime scene. Settling on the picture he wanted, Denver studied the small tattoo. As he fell farther down the rabbit hole, he signed into his computer to cross-reference the report to the dead man's digital footprint. Three hours later, and at least as many telephone calls, he had a fairly good working theory on the deceased, Jason Rice.

"Lieutenant?"

Aurora Elliott, back in uniform, trim black skirt, matching jacket flung over the back of her chair, looked up from her computer screen.

"Tell me a story," she invited.

"We received a report this morning on our cadaver. Turns out our guy had very little history. It didn't look right, so I did a little digging. There was a military tat behind his ear. That alone says he should have shown up somewhere else. Since I was striking out on the name and associated information, I decided to run him through FaceMatch. Long story short, things are not what they seem."

"Care to enlighten me, or you want me to guess?"

"I'm getting there. But, right about now," he looked at his watch, "we probably need to trot on down to the fourth floor."

"What's on the fourth floor that I would be interested in?" she asked as she stood, slinging on her jacket.

As they made their way to the elevator and took it down, he told her.

"Turns out our guy is ex-military. Instead of going to work for the trash department, he's actually undercover for Department of Defense. I have a friend of a friend of a friend…"

"Yeah, yeah…you got friends, and?"

"Turns out they have this nifty little digital camera that can be implanted into the eye. And, Jason Rice, AKA Stephen King, like the old horror writer, also had classified access to certain topside facilities due to retinal recognition. Needless to say, that makes his eye rather valuable."

"So, this wasn't a Qraven situation gone bad? Topside harvesting the organ?"

"Doubtful. Kati said something to me last night that got me thinking, and I just couldn't let it go. Why would a harvester kill him? He wouldn't."

"There's nothing on this floor but the trash department."

As they exited the elevator, a man in a dark gray suit stepped forward. He had a badge case out, and a handheld transmitter beeped in his hand.

"McNulty?" he asked.

"You with DOD? This is Lieutenant Elliott," Denver said.

"Agent Kelley," he said. "As I said on the phone, we were able to pinpoint an approximate location to this building, and on my way here, the team was able to triangulate to this floor."

Denver nodded to the agent and held out his hand to indicate they would follow. He continued his story. Kelley was still monitoring the small tracking device.

"I guess this technology is pretty expensive. Turns out they have a signal embedded in the camera, just in case anything happens to one of their operatives. Rice/King was involved in some kind of organized crime investigation being run by the DOD."

"What's the defense department's interest in the mob?" Aurora asked.

Agent Kelley scratched behind his ear. "It's a…"

"Don't give me some kind of need-to-know crap. What was this guy working on?" she demanded.

"Believe it or not, nobody pays any attention to the trash trucks. You could haul gold across the country…nuclear weapons, dead bodies…and nobody pays any attention. They have routes across the states and can move a lot of black market goods from one sky city to another. That's where the big money is, in the sky."

They stopped outside an office.

"Is this where we are going?" Denver asked Agent Kelley. The name on the door said Mickey Connors. Denver looked at his boss and shook his head.

"Leads right to this office," Kelley said. "I have agents positioned at the stairs, and exits to the building in case the tracer moved off this floor."

Denver took a deep breath and pushed open the door.

"How's it going?" Denver said in way of introduction.

Moose looked up from a pile of papers on his desk. "Denver, rare pleasure, two days in a row."

"Did you kill him in SkyIndy, Moose? Or did you kill him down here? I guess you were just going to set him out with the trash, weren't you?"

"I got no clue what you're going on about. Who, that Rice guy?"

"Really? So, you didn't know he was undercover? You took his eye. Was that to steer the investigation in the wrong direction, or because you knew he was recording your meetings?"

Moose looked surprised.

"You didn't even admit to knowing the guy last night. And, he worked for you…with SkyIndy clearance. Not many employees get topside access. It should have clued me in. I've known you for years, Moose. How can you kill somebody, then stand there and watch us process the crime scene?"

Moose chuckled, "You got the wrong guy, Denver."

"I don't think so, Moose. I wish I did."

Agent Kelley stepped into the office and his tracer increased its pulse, a quickened beep, beep, beep.

"What is this? Who is this guy?" Moose stood up in protest, and the beep led directly over to him. Kelley patted down Moose's jacket, then his slacks and removed a small glass bottle from one of the pockets, an eye clearly visible.

Moose shoved Agent Kelley with a vicious thrust of his meaty arm. Kelley's head hit the wall, and Rice's eyeball popped loose and flew into the air. Moose jumped over Kelley's falling body and darted toward the door. His dinner plate hand palmed the side of Denver's face and thrust him backwards. Denver lost his balance and toppled to the floor, flinging out a foot to try tripping Moose who sidestepped and maneuvered around him.

Aurora, looking bored, rolled her eyes. She slid a ruler-sized stick from her belt and gave the wand one strong whip. The wand extended 38 inches, then Aurora gentle poked Moose as he tried to pass through the door. Moose went down with a convulsive thud, the floor bouncing from impact.

They handcuffed Mickey Connors. The recovered eye went with DOD. Denver was left with the paperwork. And, a small bruise to his pride.

Aurora said, "You sure know how to show a girl a good time."

"There's no trash, like holiday trash." After a short pause he said, "You know anything about these bioluminaire things?"

"Bioluminescence? Like the decorations running down the halls here?" Aurora asked pointing to the flicking strands of garland hung from the ceiling panels and molded into varying shapes of Christmas ornamentation.

"No kidding? Kati has this thing she wants to do using them in her hair. How much do you know about that?" Denver snapped his fingers. "Hey you know, Kati makes a mean White Christmas Martini. How'd you like to stop by Christmas Eve?"

"Bioluminescence. It's all the rage," she smiled, "if you're seventeen."

"So, I'll see you tomorrow then?"

"Merry Christmas, Denver."

White Christmas Martini

2 ounces vanilla vodka

2 ounces white chocolate liqueur

1 ounce white crème de cacao

1 ounce half-and-half

Coarse sanding sugar

Dash of cinnamon

Pour sanding sugar in shallow dish. Dip your finger in the crème de cacao, and coat the rim of your martini glass. Set the rim in the sugar dish to coat evenly. Set the glass aside.

In a cocktail shaker filled with ice, add the vodka, white chocolate liqueur, crème de cacao, and half-and-half. Shake vigorously. Strain into the prepared martini glass. Add a dash of cinnamon.

Murder Most Merry

By Shari Held

R ichard Phillips grimaced upon seeing the Salvation Army bell ringer surrounded by Christmas carolers in front of his office building. As quickly as that emotion flitted across his face, he replaced it with a smile.

When the singers burst into "We Wish You A Merry Christmas," he reached into his coat for his wallet and dropped a ten-dollar bill into the bell ringer's kettle.

"Bless you, Sir."

Richard nodded and headed through the revolving door of the skyscraper. The lobby was resplendent with a two-story poinsettia-decorated tree, silver bows, and sparkling-white twinkle lights. Faux gift-wrapped presents were piled underneath, and holiday tunes played on a continuous loop to celebrate the season.

He took the elevator to Phillips & Associates and used his card key to enter his office. It had a view overlooking Monument Circle, the heart of the city. For the past few weeks, Sailors and Soldiers Monument had been transformed into the world's tallest Christmas tree, and shoppers, laden with holiday shopping bags, dotted the sidewalks.

Growing up, Scrooge had been Richard's idol. Still was. He didn't understand why everyone made themselves crazy buying presents they couldn't afford for people who probably didn't even appreciate them—all in the name of an oversized, mythical old man in a ridiculous red suit. A man who kept company with elves and reindeer at the North Pole, no less!

No, he didn't like Christmas one bit. But his behavior would never betray that fact. He'd learned from Scrooge's mistakes. No one would ever accuse *him* of being like the Dickens character. But he resented the price it took to pay tribute to the dratted holiday. An interior designer lavishly decorated his house and grounds. His personal shopper bought Christmas gifts for his staff, friends, and family. It all added up. Still, he kept his inner Scrooge in check and pulled no punches when it came to appearing like a benevolent uncle to his three nephews. If he'd learned anything it was that perception was everything. And he knew how to play the game with the best of them. He had one up on Scrooge when it came to that!

⁓ ⁓ ⁓

It was 5:10 p.m. on a Friday and most people had already escaped from Phillips & Associates. Nan Findley carefully shifted a stack of folders to one arm as she tapped lightly on Richard's door with her free hand. *Please don't let him be on the phone—the Pope could deliver his Christmas message quicker.*

"Come in," Richard said.

Nan opened the door and walked over to Richard's desk.

"Here are the reports you requested, Mr. Phillips." She placed them on his desk more forcefully than she'd anticipated and several pages he'd been working on flew off his desk.

Nan's cheeks turned bright red and she scurried to pick them up. "I'm so sorry, Mr. Phillips. Let me get those for you."

"Don't worry about it, Nan." Richard said. His conciliatory words didn't match the scowl on his face. Nan collected the strays and dropped them on his huge mahogany desk, trying to stack them in some semblance of order.

"Will there be anything else, Mr. Phillips?" *Please say no. Please say no.* Her heart practically stopped beating while she awaited his verdict. As a single mother with two young children, Nan rarely had any time to herself. But her children's paternal grandparents had offered to take them both for these first two weeks of December. And, miracle of miracles, she had a date for the evening.

It had happened just like a Hallmark romance. With the kids gone, Nan had decided to take in *White Christmas* on the big screen. She'd slipped and literally collided with Harry, showering him with her popcorn. They'd ended up sitting together and sharing his popcorn. Then one thing led to another. She was looking forward to tonight.

"No, I don't think so. Not tonight. But I'll need a summary of this report first thing Monday morning." He handed her a large stack of papers. "Have a nice weekend."

"You, too, Mr. Phillips." Nan didn't waste any time. She shut the door behind her and ran for her desk.

"Hey, Nan," Dylan said, glancing at the clock. "The boss is letting you off early tonight, I see. Best get out now before he changes his mind. Have a good one."

Nan flashed him a smile. Dylan was one of Mr. Phillips' three nephews. They worked at the firm during summers and school breaks. She'd gotten to know them well during the last year and was quite fond of them. "Don't worry," Nan said, grabbing her coat and purse and stuffing the papers in her oversized tote bag. "I will!"

❧ ❧ ❧

Richard leaned back in his office chair, propped his feet up on his desk, and clasped his hands behind his head. He'd have to let Nan go soon. She was becoming far too cozy with the boys. And they, with her. Too bad. She fulfilled both of his requirements for the accounting position. First, candidates had to have responsibilities that discouraged after-hour socializing with coworkers. Single mothers with young children had proven to work out quite nicely.

Second, candidates had to be efficient enough to manage the demands of the job—but not so sharp that they started asking questions. It wouldn't do for anyone to find out his dirty little secret. That's why this position was a revolving-door job. He avoided lawsuits and scenes by labeling it as a "temporary" job and paying top dollar. And if the candidate happened to be attractive like Nan, well, a little eye candy was an added bonus. Not that he'd ever indulge with an employee.

Richard didn't feel any undue remorse about what this would mean to Nan and her family, rationalizing that she knew what she was getting in to when she signed the employment agreement. In the unlikely event he did feel something akin to that emotion, he'd absolve his sins by contributing to one of his charities. No clergyman required. The large number of framed accolades hanging on his wall were a testament to his ruthless nature rather than his generosity.

Richard sat back up and glanced at his Rolex. He had to leave early to meet with the triplets and the caterers regarding the holiday party they planned to throw next Friday. He hadn't been able to persuade them to rent a public venue like The Children's Museum or one of those barns that seem to be so popular. No. They were adamant about having it at the house. While he wasn't wild about the idea, he pounced on the opportunity to piggyback off their event and invite some business acquaintances and people from work. If he didn't want them served pizza and hot dogs, he'd need to be present to ensure there were adult food choices.

One way or another the triplets would be gone next year. He couldn't wait. He glanced at the latest photo of Ryan, Bryan, and Dylan displayed on his desk. For the past ten years he'd served as their guardian—ever since their mother and father, his brother Jonathon, had died in a car crash. At least that was the story he'd told the boys. Actually, their parents had died when their car exploded as they were leaving a downtown restaurant.

Jonathan, you should have stayed with the family business. If you hadn't joined the CIA, you and Kathy would still be alive and I wouldn't have guardianship of the boys.

It wasn't totally bad, of course. The boys were the reason he'd dialed down his animosity for the holiday season. As it turned out, that was a smart career move. And the triplets were an ace up his sleeve when it came to attracting the opposite sex. Evidently no one could refuse the charm of the cherubic trio. No one but him, that is. To him they weren't so adorable. They were a liability.

෴ ෴ ෴

Nan entered St. Elmo Steakhouse on South Illinois at the stroke of eight. She hoped that didn't make her look too eager, but punctuality was her watchword. She wasn't the type that routinely allowed herself to get wined and dined by handsome strangers from Colorado. But Harry Zane, a medical device salesman, was handsome, funny, and charming—the kind of man she'd like her ex to see her with. He was just the tonic she needed after a grueling workweek. She checked her coat and gave Harry's name to the hostess who promptly escorted her to their table.

"Nan, thank you for recommending this restaurant," Harry said as he rose from his chair. "All the sizzling steaks have my taste buds standing at attention!"

"Well, they'll have to wait for the steak. You must try the world-famous shrimp cocktail. Just be careful with the sauce or your taste buds will be fried!"

The waiter stood patiently by the table. "We'll take two," Harry told him.

"If you would care for some wine with your shrimp cocktail, I recommend the 2011 Loosen Bros. Riesling by the glass."

"Great," Harry said. "And according to my date, you'd better bring a pitcher of water, too!"

Nan glowed. It had been a long time since someone had called her his date. "So how did your meeting go?" Nan asked after the waiter left.

"Promising. Thanks for asking. It helps that I have a knack for getting people to open up. So, how was your day?"

Nan hesitated before responding. "It was okay. Not as demanding as usual. It's just that..." Nan frowned and the lines between her eyes deepened. "It's nothing." She traced the rim of her glass with the index finger of her right hand.

"That doesn't sound like nothing." Harry placed her hand between both of his and looked her in the eye. His expression was sincere, his brown eyes filled with compassion. "Pretend I'm a Christmas angel and tell me what's bothering you. You'll feel better. Promise."

Something in Nan melted, and she felt an overwhelming urge to confide her fears to Harry. She couldn't spill her guts to anyone at work and her friends wouldn't understand. Besides, it wasn't as though Harry was from her world. She'd never see him again after this week. Most of all, though, it just felt right.

"From all appearances, Mr. Phillips is an outstanding citizen—a successful businessman raising his three nephews and supporting the community. But there's something not quite right about him." Nan took a big gulp of wine, then set her glass on the table.

She did a quick assessment of the nearby diners to ensure she didn't recognize anyone. Then she turned back to Harry. "I'm an accountant for the firm, but I also get stuck handling some personal things for Mr. Phillips. He has custody of his three nephews—

their parents were killed in a car crash when the boys were quite young—and since this is a family-owned business, there's overlap between personal and business. The boys have a trust, based on their father's share of the business, that Mr. Phillips manages. I was working on that today, and decided to go over the files from the very beginning..."

Nan's voice dropped even lower. "I could be wrong, but I think Mr. Phillips has been skimming money from their trust. Every month for nearly ten years, the trust has paid E. S. Associates $10,000 or more. I can't find a website or any information about the company, which is strange. But get this. I've deposited several checks from that company directly into Mr. Phillips' personal banking account. Don't you think that's damning?"

"So, what are you going to do about it? You'll have to be very sure about this before you ask him about it or mention it to anyone."

"There's more," Nan said. "Nothing I can prove. Call me crazy, but he's so greedy I worry about him harming the boys. I've seen the way he looks at them when he thinks no one's around." Nan took a deep breath. "Do you have children, Harry? If so, you can understand my concern."

Harry turned his attention to his hands. Nan wished she'd never mentioned the last bit. She could kick herself. This was becoming less of a date and more of a therapy session with each passing minute.

"I had a family once," Harry said when he looked up. "I know what it's like to do anything you can to protect your children. How does he treat the boys?"

"If you go by appearances, he's the perfect, dutiful uncle. But if you pay attention to the undercurrents when all four of them are together, the tension in the room says otherwise. Of course, everyone knows how difficult teens can be. However, given the choice, I wouldn't want Richard as my guardian. I don't think the boys do either."

Harry looked off into the distance. "How much money do you think he's stolen from their trust so far?"

"Hard to tell the extent of it. But just this one monthly transaction has netted him more than $2 million over the years. Plus, he's being paid a nice salary for managing their trust."

The waiter arrived with their shrimp cocktails and Harry ordered another round of wine by the glass, their entrees, and a bottle of Cabernet Sauvignon.

"There's something else. Now you'll really think I'm a nutcase. But I once overheard him telling someone on the phone that the boys will soon be gone. Maybe I'm reading too much into that after discovering his theft, but I'm not convinced he's talking about college." Nan's face was flushed. "And I love those boys, Harry. I'd be sick if anything happened to them. What do you think I should do? Should I tell someone what I fear based only on my intuition?"

Harry picked up his shrimp fork in anticipation of sinking it into the fiery concoction. "I wouldn't say anything to anyone for the time-being. I have a few friends who might be able to advise you. Let me ask around. For now, let's just enjoy the evening and this wonderful meal." He held up his glass, and Nan responded by clinking her glass against his.

"So, do you go to the movies often?" Harry asked.

"Yes. I love going to the movies. When I was young I used to park myself in the theater on Saturdays, going from one movie to another until I'd had so much popcorn and soda I waddled out."

Just then a waiter passed by carrying a tray of used dishes stacked so high one of the glasses hit a gold bell hung from the archway. A beautiful tinkling sound was the result.

"Another angel got its wings," Harry said.

"*It's a Wonderful Life* is my favorite Christmas movie."

"Isn't it everyone's?" Harry smiled as the waiter delivered their main course.

They finished their steaks over a lively discussion about movies that encompassed everything from *To Kill a Mockingbird* to *Cleopatra* and Christmas classics. Then they opted for dessert. Nan hadn't had this much fun in years. The ambience was all she could ask for. The restaurant was tastefully decorated with a tree adorned with white lights, red bows, and gold bells. And the meal and the company were perfection. "Okay, here's one for you," she said, loading her spoon with a bite of their shared slice of White Chocolate Blueberry Bread Pudding. "What movie began with: He was the most extraordinary man I ever knew?"

"*Lawrence of Arabia*! Wasn't that a wonderful movie? Peter O'Toole was fantastic. Here, you can have the last bite." Harry pushed the plate toward her.

"I shouldn't, but it's so good. Harry, since you're going to be in town Friday night, would you like to attend a party at Mr. Phillips' place with me? That is, if you don't have other plans. It's a combined party with the boys and their friends. It could be interesting."

Harry didn't hesitate. "I'd love to! Give me your iPhone and I'll plug in my number. It would be nice if I had your home number as well so we can confirm the details later."

After leaving St. Elmo's, Harry and Nan walked around the Circle for a close-up look at the "World's Largest Christmas Tree." Snow was falling as they watched the skaters and the colorful, horse-drawn carriages make their rounds.

"Want to go on a carriage ride, Nan?" Harry asked. "That Cinderella carriage has your name written all over it."

It was a nice treat, and the perfect way to end the night. Harry walked her to her car and kissed her lightly on the lips. His kiss tasted of red wine and white chocolate. Absolute heaven. Nan noticed it was the stroke of midnight when she pulled away from the curb. She felt every bit like a fairy princess.

⌒:∼ ⌒:∼ ⌒:∼

It was late when Harry got back to his hotel room, but he had a report to make. Despite the cold, he opened the sliding glass door and stood on the balcony.

"Hi, Chief. Just wanted to give you an update. It's exactly as I thought. Richard is ripping the boys off—and perhaps something more sinister." Harry kicked at the balcony wall, his face contorted in pain.

"I don't believe he's hurt them physically—not yet. But money is everything to him. If an opportunity presented itself to get rid of the boys without getting his hands dirty, I think he'd jump on it. Nan asked me to a party at Richard's residence Friday night. That will provide me with the perfect opportunity to have a little chat with him."

After signing off, Harry stood still in thought. What great luck. Nan had unwittingly handed him the means to see the boys and confront Richard face-to-face. In the meantime, he'd resist the urge to interfere. He took a leisurely look around the city. It had really grown since he had last lived here. The dinner at St. Elmo's was as good as always. Some things never change. Maybe he'd check out Acapulco Joe's and the Chatterbox tomorrow. On second thought, he'd try one of the newer restaurants. After all, you have to keep up with the times.

As Harry came inside, he paused in front of the mirror and stared at his reflection. He didn't look anything like he had the last time he'd been in Indy. His hair was darker and longer than he'd ever worn it. His face was thinner, with a few added wrinkles. It wasn't what he was used to, but the new look wasn't bad. Not bad at all.

⁂ ⁂ ⁂

Richard opened a pricy bottle of Sauterne he'd purchased at an auction. It was a rare and welcome find. Sauternes had been out of vogue for years, but he loved them all the same. He didn't think twice about dropping $300 for a half-bottle of Chateau d'Yquem. He poured a glass and held it up to the light before taking the first sip. This half-bottle cost more than he was spending for his guests at Friday's party. He'd opted to serve a red wine Wassail. It was, after all, traditional Christmas fare. Better yet, he'd told the caterers he'd supply the wine. It was a great way to get rid of the bottles of gifted wine he'd received that didn't meet his standards.

The boys had surprised Richard with a sophisticated menu selection. They selected mini roast beef sandwiches with horseradish sauce, shrimp cocktails, an assortment of sushi and a variety of other edibles. Plus, they were going to have pizza delivered to the basement game room where most of their festivities would take place. *Ah, well. It's their money.* Richard had volunteered to provide the alcohol for his guests while the boys paid for the food. He'd spend next to nothing and still entertain his guests in style.

That appealed to the Scrooge in him.

⁂ ⁂ ⁂

Nan checked herself in the mirror. She'd gone all out for the party. Instead of a practical little black dress, hers was bright Christmas red, with a neckline that was suggestive rather than revealing. It was the perfect foil for the one piece of decent jewelry she owned—a diamond solitaire necklace repurposed from her engagement ring.

She gathered her coat and purse and waited for Harry to arrive. They had enjoyed a wonderful meal at Tinker Street earlier in the week. It was even more fun than the St. Elmo's outing. Too bad Harry was headed back to Colorado on Saturday. He'd done a great job of spoiling her. Thanks to him she had enough fond memories to last her for a long time. More than that. Being with Harry had given her the confidence and the desire to start dating again—kids or no kids.

A knock on her door brought her back to the present. She couldn't wait to show up at the party with a handsome man at her side.

ᴄ:ᴖ ᴄ:ᴖ ᴄ:ᴖ

The intricately paneled mahogany door was open so visitors could walk in. Richard stood in the doorway between the dining room and the entry. From this vantage point he could greet guests and keep an eye on the buffet and the Wassail bowl. He'd warned the servers not to allow the kids to have any Wassail, but he didn't trust they'd be as vigilant as he was. After all, he had a reputation to protect.

The door opened and Nan walked in with a date. Richard did a double-take. Nan didn't look like the same person who sat hunched over her desk all day. And her date didn't look like someone he would have thought she'd associate with socially. His attire was impeccable—and expensive. And that sexy dress must have set Nan back a pretty penny. He was obviously paying her too much. Oh, well. He'd soon be rid of her.

"Nan. So nice you could make it," Richard said.

"Thank you for the invitation. This is my guest, Harry Zane. Harry, this is my boss, Richard Phillips."

Richard and Harry shook hands. Richard felt a slight shock, a tingling that set the hair on the back of his neck on edge. He quickly withdrew his hand. "Welcome, Mr. Zane. We have food and drink available in the dining room."

"Where are the boys?" Nan asked. "I'd like to see them before mingling with the adults."

Richard looked toward the dining room. "I don't see them at the buffet so they're probably in the game room on the lower level. The stairs are just through the dining room before you get to the kitchen."

Nan talked to a few people while Harry got them some Wassail. "Let's go see the boys. You don't mind meeting them, do you?"

"Not at all. Can you give me a heads up about them? Are they into sports? Academics? What's the scoop?"

Nan laughed. "My, but you're playing the perfect guest tonight. Most men would balk at having to spend time with three teens they'd never met before. At least you've got something to drink. How is it?"

"Not bad, actually, although I sure could use a glass of scotch right now."

Nan grabbed his arm and steered him though the dining room. "To answer some of your questions, the triplets—Ryan, Bryan, and Dylan—participate in sports. Not the usual ones like basketball or football. One's a runner, one plays tennis, and the third one's into hockey. They all hit the books and make good grades. Engineering attracts Ryan, Bryan has his heart set on becoming an architect, and Dylan's dream is to be a broadcast journalist. At least that's what I heard last week."

The boys were at the bottom of the stairs good-naturedly squabbling over what channel the TV should be on. "Boys, I have someone I want you to meet," Nan said. "This is a friend of mine from out of town, Harry Zane."

"Wow, look at you! What a Babe! Totally hot, Nan!" the boys collectively voiced their approval as they each, in turn, gave Nan a big hug. That was followed by "nice-to-meet-yous" and handshakes for Harry.

"So, guys, did you go to the Super Bowl when it was here back in 2012?" Harry asked. From then on they talked about football and other sports until their friends began to arrive. At that point Nan and Harry went back upstairs.

"You're a natural with teens," Nan said. "These kids are wonderful, but I've seen them turn into holy terrors when they thought they could get away with it." She glanced over her shoulder to see if anyone was nearby. "I think it's because they have to be so proper when Mr. Phillips is around. It can't be much fun for them."

Harry smiled, but he had a pained look in his eyes. "Would you like some more Wassail?"

"Sure. But I think I'd better have some food along with it."

"Come along with me, then, and we'll fill our plates, grab some drinks, and find a secluded nook to continue our conversation."

They talked and laughed about everything and nothing. Then Nan saw an old friend. "Harry, if you'll excuse me, I really want to catch up with Bonnie. I haven't seen her in forever, so it could take more than a couple minutes. Do you mind?"

"Not at all. I'll clean up here and take a self-guided tour of the house. Take your time."

⁓:⁓ ⁓:⁓ ⁓:⁓

Harry saw Richard leave the group he was talking to and head into the study. Harry followed, shutting the door behind him.

"Hey, what do you think you're doing?" Richard asked as he stepped toward Harry.

In response, Harry's features altered until he looked like his true self.

Richard gasped, his face white as the Christmas snow. "Jonathan? What is this? A sick joke?"

"No joke, Richard. It's me. Jonathan. Your dear, departed brother. Aren't you glad to see me?"

"But that can't be," Richard sputtered. "You're dead! You died ten years ago. You were blown to bits."

"That's true," Jonathan said.

Richard backed up, never taking his eyes off Jonathan. "We both know that isn't possible. I don't know how you did the morphing bit, but you can't be my brother. You're just some scam artist trying to get my money. Well, we'll see about that." He started to pick up the phone.

"Okay, you want some proof, little brother? When we were kids you used to pinch Dad's *Playboys* and hide in the attic behind that old monstrosity of a mirror that belonged to Great Aunt Harriet. When Mom found your cache, you told her they were mine. I was grounded for a month."

"So, is this like Dickens' *Christmas Carol*? Are you a Christmas spirit sent to warn me? Is this an intervention?"

"Not even close," Jonathan said. "What would I have to warn you about, little brother? Maybe the fact you're cheating my sons out of their inheritance? Maybe even trying to get rid of them before they can claim what's left of it? You'd like to be the sole heir, wouldn't you?"

"Anyone would like to be the sole heir to a fortune. That's just natural. That doesn't mean I'd do anything to harm the boys. Why would you even say that?"

"The dead have their ways of knowing things. To answer your previous question, no, I'm not the Spirit of Christmas Past, Present, or Yet to Come. I'm an angel—an Avenging Angel. Ironic, isn't it? Who knew I'd be able to use the skills I learned in the CIA in the afterlife."

Richard backed up even more. He placed a trembling hand on his chest. "Okay, so I dipped into the boys' funds when I shouldn't have. I can fix that. I'll put it all back—with interest. Other than that slight indiscretion I've taken excellent care of them. Even you would have to admit that. I took them to Disneyland and on vacation every summer. Saw that they were clothed and fed. I sent them to the best schools..."

"But did you really care for them? Love them like they were yours? Or did you just do your duty?"

"I, I did my best," Richard said.

"Well, you fell short. Unlike your idol Scrooge, you never changed. And you had every opportunity."

"That's not true. Scrooge was visited by three spirits. No one's visited me!"

"Remember when you had the dream about Uncle Harold? Christmas Past."

"How do you know about that? That was just an aberration brought on by indigestion. It doesn't mean anything," Richard scoffed.

"How about last month when you overheard Mrs. Hubert talk about how stingy you are? That the only thing you care more about than money is your time? Christmas Present."

"That old biddie! She's just jealous because she treated her money like an infinite resource and now it's dwindled down to nothing."

Jonathan shook his head. "Christmas Yet to Come was that little kid who pleaded with you to contribute money toward a playground for disadvantaged kids like himself. That didn't get a reaction from you either."

"Hey, that little snot-nosed kid got dirt on my Giorgio Armani wool suit!"

Jonathan continued as though he hadn't heard Richard. "So, you see, you had your warnings. Unlike Scrooge, you didn't recognize the error of your ways and change. That's when avenging angels, like me, step in. Now it's time for you to pay the price."

Jonathan stepped forward and put his hand on Richard's clammy forehead. Richard jerked, then his eyes rolled back in his head and he fell, hitting his head on the corner of the desk. Blood flowed over Richard's Persian carpet.

"Merry Christmas, little brother. Rest in peace."

Red Wine Wassail

3 cups apple cider

½ cup honey

2 quarts inexpensive (but not cheap!) red wine, preferably a Cabernet Sauvignon

1 orange—the zest and juice

2 cinnamon sticks

24 whole cloves

Garnish

Orange slices

In a crockpot combine the apple juice, honey, orange juice, and orange zest. Slowly stir in red wine.

Take a large piece of cheesecloth and place the cinnamon sticks and cloves on it. With string, tie it up to make a small bundle and drop it into the red wine mixture.

Heat on high in the crockpot for about three hours. Do not let it boil.

Discard the spice bag and pour the heated Wassail into a large punch bowl (or crock pot on low heat). Then add the orange slices. Your home will smell lovely!

Makes 12 to 16 servings

The Mysterious Mincemeat Murder

By Joan Bruce

here should we eat dinner on Christmas Eve?" my best friend, Mandy Malone, asked after I picked up my phone.

"You didn't win another Caribbean cruise?" I asked.

"Nope, my stores finished third in this year's Goodyear winter tire sales promotion. No cruise for me. Just a form letter from the company's president."

Too bad. I was hoping to go with you this year.

"So, what's it going to be? Steak or seafood?" Mandy asked.

"Let's do something different this year," I said.

"Like what?"

"Martha Rae Folger told me about an opportunity the other day when she stopped by the salon."

"What?" Mandy asked.

"The administrator at the new assisted living facility is giving her staff the night off on Christmas Eve, so they can spend time with their families before they return to work on Christmas Day. She's inviting local folks to treat her residents to a potluck dinner on Christmas Eve and a musical program."

"Wait a minute," Mandy said. "You want me to spend Christmas Eve spoon feeding some toothless old woman instead of eating dinner at an upscale restaurant in Indianapolis? No way."

"Mandy, don't be such a Scrooge," I said. "It'll be fun. Helping the less fortunate is what Christmas is all about. Besides, we shouldn't be filling our faces with food that isn't on our diets. And, we'll get to sing Christmas carols to the residents. I love to sing."

"The only singing I do is in my shower."

"Martha Rae plans to interview the volunteers on her radio show all week."

"She does?" Mandy asked.

"Yeah, and whoever donates the turkey and ham for the dinner will be mentioned several times on her show."

"Maybe volunteering at the Springs isn't such a bad idea," Mandy said. "After all, if Martha Rae is behind it, everyone in town will know about it, right?"

"Right," I said. "So, you're willing to help?"

"Why not. People need to know my business supports the less fortunate."

"Great. There's just one more thing," I said. "I want Emma Lou Pettijohn to join us."

"Who?"

"Emma Lou," I said. "Remember, she's the older woman I ate Christmas Eve dinner with last year when you were on your cruise."

"Is she the one who kept stealing the naked baby Jesus from the manger at First United Methodist Church because she thought he'd catch pneumonia?"

"Yes. I've already talked to her about that. She's promised to leave him alone this year if the church ladies wrap him in a warm blanket."

∾∶∾ ∾∶∾ ∾∶∾

It was nearing six o'clock when Mandy and I picked up Emma Lou in front of her gigantic, two-story Victorian house on East Washington Street and drove her to the Springs of Bartonsville. Margaret Sullivan, the facility's administrator, greeted us at the main entrance.

"Good evening, ladies," she said with a big smile. "What have you brought us?"

"A pre-cooked turkey breast and a spiral ham," Mandy said, pointing to the heavy bags in my arms. "You'll need to warm them in an oven for a few minutes."

"And, what did you bring?" Ms. Sullivan said, turning to Emma Lou.

"A tray of mincemeat tarts," she proudly replied. "I made them myself, using my mother's old English recipe."

"How interesting," Ms. Sullivan said. "I've never eaten one before. Let's put them on the dessert table in the dining room."

As we followed behind Ms. Sullivan and Emma Lou, I turned to Mandy and whispered, "What a beautiful place. I'd love to live here when I get older."

"Save the tips from your manicures, and who knows," Mandy replied. "Someday, this could be all yours."

༈ ༈ ༈

The potluck dinner went off without too many problems. For a bunch of frail-looking old people, the residents had some hearty appetites with many requesting seconds. It was as if they hadn't eaten in a week.

Mandy spent her time asking folks how they enjoyed the turkey and ham that she brought for the dinner. It was like she'd been transported back in time to when she would schmooze her diners as the hostess at the Barton County Country Club.

Martha Rae remained in the kitchen, helping Ms. Sullivan prepare bowls of vegetables and mashed potatoes and slicing the meat.

I ran between the kitchen and dining room delivering platters of meat and bowls of food to each table. Emma Lou followed behind me like a little puppy dog.

"Is everyone finished with their dinners?" Martha Rae asked after I'd returned to the kitchen for what seemed like the umpteenth time.

"I sure hope so," I said. "My feet are killing me. I haven't been a waitress for a few years. I'm out of shape."

Just then, we heard loud shrieks coming from the dining room. We ran out of the kitchen and noticed a white-haired gentleman dressed in a tweed jacket, white shirt and wearing an ugly Christmas tie, lying on the floor. He had been sitting at a table full of women and apparently had fallen out of his chair. I knelt beside him and felt for a pulse.

"He's dead," I said as I stood up a few seconds later.

"What?" Ms. Sullivan shouted. "That's impossible! Mr. Worthington can't be dead. He's one of my healthiest residents."

The ladies at the table suddenly began screeching all at once. It took a few minutes for me to quiet them down.

"Mandy, call the cops and let them know what's happened," I said. "Ms. Sullivan, send your residents back to their apartments except the ones sitting with Mr. Worthington."

"What should I do?" Martha Rae asked.

"You're a radio host," I replied. "Take Emma Lou and these ladies to the far corner of the dining room and ask them what made Mr. Worthington keel over."

"The cops are on their way," Mandy said as we watched Martha Rae and the ladies walk away. "Think the old guy had a heart attack or a stroke?"

"I don't know," I replied. "But if he was as healthy as Ms. Sullivan said, something's definitely not right here."

∾ ∾ ∾

Nate Sloan and Frank Turner of the Bartonsville Police Department arrived at the assisted-living facility within five minutes of Mandy's call.

"What are you two doing here?" Nate asked when he spotted us.

"We served the residents dinner until this guy on the floor keeled over and died," I said.

"Who is he?" Frank asked.

"All I know is that his name is Geoffrey Worthington and he was eating dinner with a bunch of ladies," I replied. "Where's Chief Cobb?"

"Dan drove to Indianapolis for the holidays, but we'll call and get him back here right away," Nate said. "I'll also call the coroner."

"Where are the women who were sitting with this guy?" Frank asked.

"Talking to Martha Rae," I said, pointing to the far corner of the dining room.

"Oh, great, that's all we need is her nosing around in the middle of everything," Frank replied. "It's liable to end up on her radio show."

Frank and Nate walked over to Martha Rae, said something briefly to her and Emma Lou, before they began interviewing the women themselves.

"What did Nate and Frank say?" I asked when Martha Rae and Emma Lou returned to where we were standing.

"They told us to mind our own business and stay out of their investigation," Martha Rae said.

"And, those nasty women said Geoffrey died after eating one of my mincemeat tarts," Emma Lou said.

~:~ ~:~ ~:~

It took me, Mandy, and Martha Rae at least a half hour to calm down Emma Lou and persuade her that her mincemeat tarts couldn't possibly have killed Mr. Worthington even though someone kept yelling that the tarts were poisoned. The breakthrough came when I agreed to eat one of them myself.

I know. What was I thinking?

"Are you crazy?" Mandy said as she followed me to the dessert table. "You could drop dead just like that old guy. Who knows what your friend put in her tarts."

"Listen, I trust that she followed her Mom's recipe," I said, placing a tart on a small plate and returning to the dinner table. Once there, I took a tiny bite of the tart. The pastry was very flaky. The ingredients thick and fruity.

"What's in this tart?" I asked Emma Lou, taking a second bite.

"Raisins, currants, lemon zest, shredded suet, chopped mixed peel, brown sugar and a touch of nutmeg," she replied.

"Is that all?"

"My mother's recipe calls for brandy, but the jar of mincemeat I bought at the store was non-alcoholic, so I added my own alcohol."

"Wait a minute," Mandy said. "That tart is laced with alcohol? Let me taste it."

"But, a minute ago you were afraid for me to try it," I said. "What changed your mind?"

"It contains alcohol?" Mandy said, grabbing the tart out of my hand and taking a big bite.

"Emma Lou, this is delicious," Mandy said. "I need a tart of my own." She stood up and headed for the dessert table.

As I looked up, I noticed Dr. William Armstrong enter the dining room. He's been a general practice physician in Bartonsville and the county's coroner for a hundred years. My mom took me to him when I was a kid.

Nate and Frank spoke briefly to him before steering the doctor to the dead guy. I waited a few minutes before I wandered over to where Dr. Armstrong was examining the body.

"What did he die of?" I asked.

"Who are you?"

"Candi DeCarlo," I replied. "I was a patient of yours when I was a kid. And, I'm the one who checked his pulse after he fell over."

"That was very brave of you, Ms. DeCarlo," Dr. Armstrong said. "Most people won't go anywhere near a dead person. I won't know what caused his death until I get him back to the morgue and can perform a more thorough exam."

"Well?" Mandy asked when I returned to the table.

"Doc doesn't know what caused Mr. Worthington's death," I said. "Maybe he was allergic to an ingredient in the tart. Like kids who get sick from eating peanut butter. Or, maybe he was allergic to the brandy."

"That's a horrible thought," Mandy said.

Dr. Armstrong spent another half hour examining Mr. Worthington before he released his body to the paramedics. After they had all left, Nate and Frank approached our table.

"Got anything more to say about what happened tonight?" Nate asked.

"No," I replied. "We were in the kitchen when Mr. Worthington keeled over. We didn't see anything."

"Are you done interviewing the residents?" Martha Rae asked.

"For now," Frank said. "We'll return tomorrow if Dr. Armstrong's autopsy raises any new questions. Chief Cobb also should be back in town by then."

As Nate and Frank left, Margaret Sullivan walked up to our table.

"Get your residents calmed down?" I asked.

"I hope so," Ms. Sullivan replied. "I'm actually more concerned about their children once word gets out about Mr. Worthington's death. They'll want to move their parents to a safer facility."

"Sorry to hear that," I said. "So, what should we do now?"

"Let's help Margaret clean the kitchen, so her staff doesn't have a mess when they return to work tomorrow," Martha Rae said.

"Excellent idea," Mandy said, biting into another mincemeat tart. "Candi and Emma Lou can straighten the dining room while the rest of us work in the kitchen."

⁓ ⁓ ⁓

"Did you know any of the women sitting with Mr. Worthington?" I asked Emma Lou as we wiped down the tables in the dining room.

"Mildred McDonald," Emma Lou replied. "Our husbands were once business partners. The four of us would get together regularly to play bridge, but after our husbands passed away, Mildred and I drifted apart."

"What was her theory about Mr. Worthington dying?" I asked.

"She thinks it was my mincemeat tart," Emma Lou replied. "He either choked on it or it poisoned him."

"She said that to your face?" I said. "I thought you'd been friends for years."

"Her comment really wasn't aimed at me," Emma Lou said. "It was more a statement of disappointment."

"What do you mean?"

"Geoffrey Worthington was considered a prized catch."

"Huh?"

"Not many men live here," Emma Lou said. "Geoffrey was a recent widower. He was handsome and appeared to be in good health. My guess is several women had their eyes on him."

"They wanted to marry him?"

"No, silly, just looking for a roll in the hay."

"Oh," I said, my face suddenly turning red. "Think Mildred killed Mr. Worthington?"

"Doubt it, she loved her husband, Edgar, too much," Emma Lou said. "Besides, he left her a fortune. Mildred wouldn't be interested in squandering it on another man."

"Did she have any other suspects in mind besides you?"

"If she did, Mildred wasn't about to say anything in front of the others," Emma Lou said. "These women wouldn't let a man—even a dead one—get in the way of their friendships."

"Maybe we should talk to her privately," I said. "Since Mandy and I didn't die after eating your tarts, I doubt Mr. Worthington was poisoned, but who knows. Nate and Frank didn't seem to have any clue about what happened to him or have a suspect in mind. Maybe, we can figure it out on our own."

"That sounds wonderful," Emma Lou said. "I've always wanted to be a detective likes the ones on TV."

We walked to the facility's main entrance where Emma Lou and I found Mildred McDonald's mailbox and the number of her apartment. It took us only a few minutes to locate her place. We gently knocked on her door.

A minute went by before a short, white-haired woman in a pink satin housecoat opened her door.

"What are you doing here, Emma Lou?" Mildred McDonald asked.

"My friend, Candi, and I want to ask you a few questions about tonight," Emma Lou said. "Can we come in?"

"I guess so, but I don't know what more I can tell you," Mildred said, opening her door wider to let us inside. Her apartment was gorgeous. She'd obviously spent part of Edgar's money buying some expensive furniture. It put my apartment to shame. Emma

Lou and I sat on a large floral-patterned sofa in the living room. Mildred sat across from us in a straight-back chair.

"Emma Lou says you think Mr. Worthington either choked to death on one of her mincemeat tarts, or he was poisoned," I said. "Is that correct?"

"That's what I said," Mildred replied.

"Sorry, but I don't think he choked to death," I said. "When I knelt beside him to check his pulse, his mouth was clear. No sign of the tart stuck in his mouth or throat. Ms. Sullivan says he was her healthiest resident, so while a heart attack is certainly possible, I'm guessing that didn't cause his death. That leaves poisoning."

"Why do you think he was poisoned, Mildred?" Emma Lou asked. "Know something you're not telling us?"

"Of course not," Mildred said. "I don't know. It just popped into my head. I was watching a *Law and Order* rerun before dinner. A woman was accused of poisoning her husband for his insurance money. The episode must have stuck with me."

Emma Lou turned to me and rolled her eyes.

"Mildred, what do you remember right before Mr. Worthington collapsed on the floor?" I asked.

"Geoffrey was finishing the last bite of his dinner when I jumped up and headed to the dessert table. He was a very proper Englishman, so I figured he knew all about mincemeat tarts and would enjoy one for dessert. Betty Foster and Vivian Appleton apparently had the same idea. Suddenly the three of us were each grabbing a tart and a small plate and rushing back to the table."

"Whose tart did Geoffrey eat?" Emma Lou asked.

"I don't know," Mildred replied. "I slipped on the carpet underneath the dessert table on my way back. By the time I got to the dinner table, Geoffrey had bitten into a tart. I don't know if it was Betty's or Vivian's."

"What can you tell us about Betty and Vivian?" I asked.

"They're gold diggers," Mildred said with a straight face. "A single man doesn't stand a chance around that pair. They're all over the poor guy until they find out he either isn't rich or can't perform where it counts."

"What was Mr. Worthington's situation?" Emma Lou asked.

"Everyone figured he was wealthy, but Geoffrey hadn't been here long enough for anyone to know if he was a player," Mildred said.

"A player?" I asked.

"Yeah, you know, a guy who enjoys women fussing over him."

"Sounds like we should chat with Betty and Vivian," Emma Lou said.

"I agree." I said.

Emma Lou and I thanked Mildred for her time and headed to the apartments of the two gold diggers. Mildred had given us their numbers.

"Still think Mr. Worthington was poisoned?" Emma Lou asked.

"I don't know," I replied. "But I'm guessing if he was allergic to an ingredient in your tarts, he wouldn't have eaten it. He would know. After all, he was an Englishman, right?"

"Right."

Betty Foster's apartment was three doors down from Mildred's place. We knocked several times, but there was no response.

"Suppose she's already asleep?" I asked.

"Doubt it," Emma Lou responded. "If she's like most old women, she can't sleep at night and likely stays up watching TV or reading a book."

I glanced at my Betty Boop watch.

"It's approaching nine o'clock," I said. "Maybe we should check on Vivian."

Her place was on the other side of the facility. It took us ten minutes to walk there. A huge Christmas wreath covered her door, making it hard to find a clear space to knock.

A minute went by before a tall woman with rust-colored hair opened her door and asked what we wanted.

"We want to ask you about Mr. Worthington," I said. "Can we come in?"

Vivian invited us into her living room. Another woman was already sitting in a chair.

"This is my friend, Betty Foster," Vivian said. "Who are you two?"

"I'm Candi and this is Emma Lou," I said. "We helped serve you dinner tonight."

"I thought you looked familiar," Betty said. "What can we do for you?"

"You were sitting with Geoffrey Worthington and each offered him a mincemeat tart for dessert, is that right?" I said.

"So?" Vivian said.

"What do you think happened to Geoffrey?" Emma Lou said. I could tell she was still smarting from Mildred's comment about her tart poisoning him.

"Poor Geoffrey wasn't poisoned like Mildred thinks," Vivian said. "She has an overactive imagination. She watches too many cop shows on TV."

"What about you, Betty?" I asked.

She shrugged and didn't say anything.

Emma Lou and I continued questioning Betty and Vivian, but they didn't have any more insights into Mr. Worthington's death. I wondered if they were hiding something. Emma Lou and I were about to leave when I asked Vivian if I could use her bathroom.

"It's at the end of the hall," she said.

After relieving myself, I washed my hands and looked in the mirror above her sink. I looked awful. Trudy Castle and I worked on clients until nearly five o'clock. Our boss, Madge Parsons, doesn't believe in closing Tips & Toes early, even on Christmas Eve.

I was about to turn and leave when I was suddenly overcome by a desire to peek inside Vivian's medicine cabinet.

The devil made me do it.

Amid several bottles of perfume, mascara, and tubes of lipstick was a small dark bottle. I picked it up.

"Sodium cyanide?" I said aloud as I read the label. "What's Vivian doing with it?"

I didn't wait to answer my own question. I needed to get back to the living room before everyone wondered why I was lingering in the bathroom.

"Is everything okay?" Vivian asked as I sat down on her couch next to Emma Lou.

"Fine," I said, trying not to look too guilty.

Emma Lou and I stayed a few more minutes before we excused ourselves and left Vivian's apartment.

"Find anything interesting in Vivian's bathroom?" Emma Lou asked as we walked back to the facility's dining room.

"Why'd you say that?" I asked.

"Vivian and Betty were wondering what was taking you so long in there," Emma Lou said.

"I found a bottle of sodium cyanide in Vivian's medicine cabinet," I said. "She might have used it to poison Geoffrey."

It was another five minutes before Emma Lou and I returned to the dining room. Mandy, Martha Rae and Margaret Sullivan were sitting at a table each enjoying a cup of coffee.

"Where have you two been?" Mandy asked. "We were worried about you."

"Candi and I did a little detective work of our own," Emma Lou said.

"What?" Martha Rae said.

I told them how after meeting Emma Lou's old friend, Mildred

McDonald, we ended up visiting Betty Foster and Vivian Appleton.

"Not those two," Margaret said when I finished.

"Why'd you say that?"

"They're the two residents who cause me the most grief."

"How so?" I asked.

"They're constantly competing to see which one can attract the most men in this place," Margaret said. "They both viewed Geoffrey as a huge prize."

"Who was winning?" Mandy asked

"Neither, I'm afraid," Margaret said. "Geoffrey was still in mourning over his wife's death and wasn't interested in a female companion, and especially not Betty or Vivian."

"What makes you so sure?" Martha Rae asked.

"He came to my office last week. Asked me to speak to them. He wanted to be left alone. I spoke to Betty and Vivian two days ago."

"Maybe they were still angry at your meeting," I said. "But, was that enough to want to see Mr. Worthington dead?"

"Hard to say," Margaret replied, taking another sip of her coffee. "They're very competitive and they don't like to take `no' for an answer."

"Can I ask another question?" I said. "What did Vivian's husband do for a living?"

"Her last one was a pharmacist," Margaret said. "Owned his own independent pharmacy before he passed away."

I stood up and started to walk away.

"Where are you going now?" Mandy said.

"I'm calling the cops," I said. "I know who poisoned Geoffrey Worthington."

༄༅ ༄༅ ༄༅

"What's going on?" Nate Sloan and Frank Turner asked after entering the Springs of Bartonsville dining room a half hour later.

"Candi knows who poisoned Geoffrey Worthington," Emma Lou said.

"She does, does she?" Frank said. "Interfering in police business again, Candi? Hasn't Chief Cobb already warned you to mind your business when it comes to police matters?"

"Yes," I said. "But, I'm pretty sure I've got the right person this time."

"Let's hear it then," Nate said.

I explained how Emma Lou and I visited Betty Foster and Vivian Appleton and how I accidently found a bottle of sodium cyanide in Vivian's medicine cabinet.

"So, now you're now convinced this Vivian woman poisoned Worthington," Frank asked.

"Yup."

"What makes you so sure, Candi?" Nate asked.

"Margaret says Vivian's husband was a pharmacist before he passed away."

"What do you think, Frank?" Nate said. "Should we check out Candi's story?"

"Why not," Frank said. "We've got nothing better to do tonight. It beats riding around town in a squad car with a busted heater."

Emma Lou and I gave Nate and Frank directions to Vivian's apartment.

"You should all go home and leave the police work to us," Frank said as he and Nate walked away.

"Should we leave like they said?" Mandy asked.

"No," the rest of us shouted.

ᵔᘛ ᵔᘛ ᵔᘛ

It was another hour before Nate and Frank returned to the dining room with Betty Foster and Vivian Appleton in tow.

"Was I right about the murderer?" I asked proudly.

"No," Frank replied. "You had the wrong person."

"What?"

"As we questioned them about Mr. Worthington's death, Ms. Foster broke down and confessed to poisoning him," Nate said. "She was afraid he liked Vivian more. And, if she couldn't have him, Betty didn't want Vivian to win his heart."

"She stole the bottle of sodium cyanide out of my medicine cabinet," Vivian said. "Here I thought we were best friends. And, she put it back tonight before you showed up at my apartment. Now that I think about it, you must have peeked in my cabinet, too."

Vivian looked directly at me, but I began admiring her house slippers and didn't say anything.

"What's going to happen now?" Martha Rae asked.

"We're taking Ms. Foster into custody tonight. We will meet with Chief Cobb and the coroner in the morning to decide if Mr. Worthington was in fact poisoned before we charge her with anything," Frank said.

"Make sure Chief Cobb knows I helped solve your case," I said.

"I'm sure he'll want to issue you a citizen's commendation once he finds out," Frank said as he grabbed Betty Foster's arm and headed for the main entrance.

"What should we do now?" Emma Lou asked after they left.

"I don't know about the rest of you, but I'm going home," Martha Rae said. "I'm beat."

"Us, too," said Margaret Sullivan and Vivian Appleton.

"What about us?" Mandy asked.

"I've got an idea," Emma Lou said.

"What?" I asked.

"Let's attend midnight services at First United Methodist Church," Emma Lou said. "I was so busy making mincemeat tarts the past few days that I didn't check on baby Jesus."

"Speaking of mincemeat tarts," Mandy said as we left the assisted-living facility. "Are there any left?"

Mincemeat Tart

Mincemeat

2 large sweet apples, peeled, cored and diced

1 large orange, zested, peeled and diced

1 cup raisins

1/2 cup golden raisins

1/2 cup dried apricots, chopped

1/3 cup dark brown sugar

1/4 cup lemon juice

1/2 teaspoon cinnamon

1/2 teaspoon nutmeg

1/2 teaspoon allspice

1/2 cup brandy (Or, as Emma Lou reminds us: "Any strong liquor will do.")

Pastry

1 1/4 cups all-purpose flour

1/2 teaspoon salt

1 tablespoons granulated white sugar

1/2 cup cold unsalted butter, cut into 1-inch chunks

3 to 4 tablespoons ice cold water

In a medium saucepan, mix diced apples, orange zest, diced orange fruit, and remaining ingredients except the brandy. Stir and simmer over medium heat, stirring occasionally for 30 minutes. Remove the mixture from the heat and stir in the brandy. Place the mixture in an air-tight container and store in the refrigerator for at least 2 weeks before using, to let the flavors meld. This will keep in the fridge 2 to 3 months.

In a food processor, place the flour, salt, and sugar and process until combined. Add the cold butter and process until the mixture resembles coarse crumbs (about 15 seconds). Sprinkle about 3 tablespoons of ice water over the pastry and process just until the pastry holds together when pinched. Add a little more water, if necessary.

Turn the dough onto your work surface and gather into a ball. Divide the pastry in half, flatten each half into a disk, cover with plastic wrap, and refrigerate for 30 to 60 minutes, or until firm.

Preheat your oven to 400°F. Have ready a 24 mini muffin tin (preferably non-stick).

After pastry has chilled sufficiently, take one of the disks of pastry, and place on a lightly floured surface. Roll out each round of pastry until it's about 1/8 inch thick. Using a round cookie cutter that's slightly bigger than the muffin cups, cut the pastry into 24 rounds. (To prevent the pastry from sticking to the counter and to ensure uniform thickness, keep lifting and turning the pastry a quarter turn as you roll (always roll from the center of the pastry outwards).)

Gently place the rounds into the muffin cups and top with a heaping teaspoon of mincemeat. Gather up any leftover scraps of pastry and re-roll. Cut out 24 stars or other shapes using a small cookie cutter, and gently place the stars on top of the mincemeat. Brush the tops of the stars with a little cream and sprinkle with granulated sugar. Bake for about 10 to 15 minutes or until the pastry is lightly browned. Remove from oven and cool on a wire rack. Dust each tart with powdered sugar before serving. Serve warm, at room temperature or cold. They can be frozen.

Makes 24 2-inch tarts.

Killer Christmas

By Janet Williams

n out-of-key Jingle Bells ringtone jolted me out of a deep sleep and I flailed as I grabbed my phone from the nightstand. "Jake" flashed on the screen in my darkened room.

"What the hell, Jake," I sputtered.

"Oh Annie, is it really you?" The voice was ragged and frantic, not sounding at all like my cool, always-in-command partner.

"Jake? What is it? What's wrong?" I asked, anxiety rising as I struggled to sit upright.

"You've got to come down to the coroner's office now and see this."

"See what? What's going on?"

"Just come. Doc and I will meet you here." He clicked off, leaving me to stare at my phone for a long moment, trying to understand what just happened.

Jake and I had solved a string of murders, making the department and the chief look good. Really good. Our reward was two weeks off at Christmas. Didn't we at least deserve to get through the holiday before the next big case? I checked the phone. It wasn't even 4 a.m.

I threw on the jeans that lay crumpled on the floor and the sweater I had tossed over a chair after I got in from last night's Christmas party. Ah, party. That's why my head throbbed and my stomach churned. One too many glasses of holiday cheer.

After popping a couple of aspirin and brushing my teeth, I tied my straggly hair into a ponytail and left. I lived in downtown Indianapolis just a few blocks from the public safety building so I walked, hoping the brisk night air would help clear my head.

I used my ID to get through the electronic front door and made my way to the basement, home to the morgue. I pushed my way through the glass doors to see Jake in an animated discussion with Tracy Bottinger. Or Doc Tracy as we affectionately called her.

Jake's eyes lit up as they caught mine and he rushed to me, wrapping me in a tight embrace. He pressed my face so tightly into his flabby chest that I could barely breathe but I could still catch the faint scent of cigarettes on his leather jacket. Smoking again.

"Thank God, thank God, thank God," he gasped.

With one limp hand I patted him on the back and with the other I pulled myself from his hold.

"Jake, what's wrong?" He was deathly pale and his eyes were puffy and red.

"See, I told you it couldn't possibly be her," he said, grabbing my arm and dragging me toward Doc like I was a mannequin.

"I can see that," Doc said, a puzzled expression on her face.

I jerked my arm away from Jake. "You high or something?"

He sighed, looking from Doc and then back to me.

"You got to see this for yourself," he said. Jake waited a second for Doc to nod her OK—this was her space, after all—and then ushered me through the thick metal doors.

I sprinted to keep up with Jake, who was a good five inches taller than me, as he loped down the corridor. He slammed through the doors leading to Doc's autopsy chamber. I knew this route well, especially after that last case when Jake and I were here every couple of days as the bodies piled up.

Jake flicked on the lights, three overhead banks of glaring fluorescent bulbs. I squinted and took a moment to focus on the exam table positioned in the middle of the cavernous room as I breathed in that antiseptic scent.

The far wall looked like the drawers of a giant file cabinet, except they were refrigerated, holding bodies until they could be autopsied, identified, or shipped off to a funeral home. A simple string of garland hanging over the wall of drawers and a small tabletop tree with blinking red and green lights gave the only hint that this was Christmas week.

"Looks like you almost got a full house," I said to Doc as I noticed that of the six drawers five had tags on them indicating a body was inside. "Busy week? Killing spree?"

Doc sighed. "We almost always end up with more than we can handle around the holidays. And except for this one here, no new business for you guys." She nodded toward the table where the body was covered by a white sheet.

Doc, who stood nearly as tall as Jake in her heeled boots, pushed ahead of him, reaching the body before he could lift the sheet.

"Let me," she said, making it clear that Jake was overstepping his boundaries.

"Annie, you're not going to believe..." Jake started to say before he was cut off by Doc's angry glare.

"Anne, prepare yourself for this." Doc's tone was so grave that my stomach did a flip-flop.

I held my breath as she lifted the sheet gently, as if she were removing a sacred shroud to show me the body of a middle-aged... no, make that late middle-aged woman. She looked vaguely familiar, about my height of five-six and with a splotchy complexion and graying short-cropped hair. Her eyes were bulging out of their sockets and the deep bruising around her neck told me she had been strangled.

As I looked at the body, from her neck to the mid-section

showing a bit of a bulge and to the bare feet, I wondered what the fuss was all about. Unless there was something about the unusual greenish gray two-piece polyester uniform. It had gold epaulets and an insignia on the left breast pocket that looked like the Indianapolis skyline hovering on the horizon, only the skyline had a tower with a flying saucer-like disc balancing on a needlepoint.

I pulled out my cellphone and snapped a photo of the insignia as Jake and Doc stared at me, expecting some kind of reaction.

"You guys know this person? Is this someone I'm supposed to know?" I asked, searching their faces to understand why they were behaving so strangely.

"You don't see it?" Jake asked.

"You mean this weird uniform? I mean, who has an insignia like this?" I asked. "We know anybody who wears these things?"

"The face! I mean the face!" Jake said. He sounded exasperated and I couldn't understand why.

I had concentrated on the strangulation marks, assuming that's what Jake and Doc wanted me to pay attention to. At the police academy I had excelled in forensics, which is why I thought for a moment there must be something unique about this particular case.

And then I saw it. I should have seen it all along, but I was distracted by the weird costume and the facial contortions caused by the choking. The shape of the face, the nose slightly upturned, the unnaturally long earlobes.

"She looks, she looks just like my mother." My voice, normally more of an alto, squeaked as it jumped an octave. Or she looked as I imagined my mother would have looked like had she lived past forty-two.

"Mother hell! She's a dead ringer for you," Jake said. Doc nodded as I looked from Jake to her.

I looked at the body more closely. Yes, I could see a resemblance, but with my mother, not me.

"She's at least twenty, thirty years older than me. And that hair." I shook the ponytail that held back my shoulder-length light brown hair. I looked nothing like this aging, out-of-shape woman on the table before me.

And yet, as I examined her face, touched her cold hand, this woman had a familiarity I couldn't explain.

"What's this? What happened here?" I asked as I examined her hand. Her fingertips had been burned off, leaving bloodied scars.

"Exactly what it looks like. Someone destroyed her prints," Jake said.

"You thought this person was me?" My tone was sarcastic and as we stood looking at the one hundred and twenty-first homicide victim of the year, I realized this wasn't a moment for sarcasm.

"I wasn't exactly thinking straight when I saw the body and yes, she reminded me of you," he said.

I studied Jake and Doc, wondering how well they knew me. We had been working together for two years, ever since I made the homicide squad and was partnered with Jake Porter, a fifty-something veteran of the unit. Dr. Tracy Bottinger had been the coroner for as long as I could remember and over time we had become good friends.

"Look at how out of shape she is." I threw my shoulders back to show off my lean, muscular figure.

"It's not just the face, Anne," Doc said as she pulled down the pants to reveal a scar on the left thigh. It was an old wound and appeared to be sinking into the flesh.

I looked closely at the scar and then at the woman's face before taking two wobbly steps back from the table. Jake took my arm, steadying me. I couldn't breathe. I couldn't speak.

The scar was the size of an elongated silver dollar with jagged edges. Just like mine. I'd been a beat cop three years ago when I was called to back up detectives who were investigating a drug house on College near 38th when one of the suspects began shooting. I was hit and the bullet tore through the fleshy part of my thigh, leaving me with an ugly scar. Jake was one of the detectives and had been the first to visit me at the hospital.

"You can't blame him for thinking it was you," Doc said.

"Sorry, Jake." The words stuck in my throat as I struggled to process what lay on the table before me. "Any idea who this person might be?" It was a lame question, but I didn't know what else to say.

"No ID. And, as you can see, no prints," Doc said.

No prints, no ID. This was turning out to be one hell of a Christmas morning.

~:~ ~:~ ~:~

That was how I ended up working a homicide on what was supposed to be my first Christmas off in ten years. We knew nothing about the woman except that she was killed about an hour before the body was discovered at the police entrance of the City-County Building. Doc would have more detailed information when she did the autopsy first thing in the morning.

A few hours later, when I was supposed to be on my way to my sister's in Columbus, Ohio, I was in our office in downtown Indianapolis. Another Christmas dinner with Marie Callender. I sighed.

Jake, who was reviewing the video from the entrance to the building, heard me and looked up. "Would you rather DiNucci or Garrett take the lead?"

I shook my head. "Those assholes? Not on your life."

"Here, take a look at this. I don't see anything," Jake said, turning his computer screen to face me.

I watched the thirty seconds of video showing two dark-clad, hooded figures carry an oversized bundle to the door, huddle for a few seconds, and then scurry away. The flickering images revealed little except that they were of average height and build.

"Security cameras get a vehicle? They couldn't have carried her very far."

Jake shook his head. "I pulled video from the street cams for three blocks in all directions and nothing. Either these guys carried her a good distance or they knew how to avoid the cameras."

"Maybe Doc will find something."

"I hope so."

While we were waiting for Doc and the autopsy results, Jake checked traffic cameras throughout the downtown area and I reviewed missing persons reports. Maybe some family member somewhere was wondering why our victim hadn't shown up for Christmas. Again, nothing.

As I considered what to do next, Doc appeared in the doorway.

"You got something for us? Anything that tells us who she is?" Jake asked.

"Nothing definitive. Cause of death, strangulation, probably manual," Doc said. "She was about your height, Anne, a few pounds heavier. She had at least one child. And she could be anywhere from mid-50s to mid-60s. Hard to tell."

"No good news? Nothing to go on?" Jake asked.

"I'm getting to it. I did find some skin fragments under the nails of her right hand. She could have scratched her killer," Doc said. "I'm going to have DNA run on that and on her. Maybe that will help us figure out who she is. And Anne, would you mind if I get a swab from you, too? Just to be sure she isn't some distant relative?"

She wanted my DNA? I was going to resist, but relented because I knew very little about my mother or her side of the family. That aged doppelganger might turn out to be a distant relative.

Doc took a cheek swab and sent the samples to the state police lab. They wouldn't begin working on the samples until tomorrow or the next day because of the holiday so we would have at least a two or three-day wait for results.

⌒∶∼ ⌒∶∼ ⌒∶∼

That evening at home as I picked over my microwave turkey and dressing, I plugged the photo of the dead woman into a Google search program. Hundreds of images popped onto the screen, most of women sleeping or lying in repose. I slowly advanced through the photos, finding nothing that resembled the woman until a picture of me appeared. As I compared my image to the visage of the dead woman I saw how much she really did look like me, from the angular jaw to the wide-set eyes, except hers were closed. Another dead end or at least that is what I kept telling myself as more photos of me from Facebook and other sites flashed across my screen.

Next, I ran the picture of the insignia through the program and quickly hundreds of images appeared. Some took me to the Space Needle in Seattle or the CN Tower in Toronto. A few images of the Indianapolis skyline showed up minus the odd structure from the insignia. Dozens of logos for businesses, sports teams and other organizations appeared in the mix, though none exactly matched the photo.

I thought I reached another dead end when an image that mirrored the needle with a flying saucer appeared. I clicked on it and as the image—a drawing, really—materialized, I spotted tiny lettering in the bottom right corner. I clicked to enlarge it and although the letters were grainy, the words were clear—Reichl Inc. The name sounded vaguely familiar but I couldn't quite place it so I started another search, this time landing on a news story about an entrepreneur launching a tech startup in a dying west side neighborhood. He had purchased an old factory and thirty acres of property a couple of years ago, erected a fence and had security guards posted there, but didn't say much about his plans. There was another story, from about six months ago, about the bodies of a man and woman discovered outside the fence. That's where I remembered the Reichl name from—Garrett and DiNucci landed that case.

I saved the article as well as a link to ReichlInc.net, the website of entrepreneur Jeffrey Reichl. Maybe the woman worked for him and the insignia was part of some kind of uniform. But the site itself contained nothing but the spaceship drawing on the home page, and when I tried to click past it I reached a login page. I played around for a few minutes trying to get past the firewall, but stopped when a security alert popped up.

I dumped my half-eaten dinner in the trash and poured myself a glass of a cheap cabernet and settled in to at least get a little Christmas spirit as I watch my favorite holiday film, *Christmas in Connecticut*.

"Merry Christmas," I said as I raised my glass to the TV when the movie credits rolled.

⌒⁞∾ ⌒⁞∾ ⌒⁞∾

Two days later Jake and I had followed every lead and ended up with nothing more than what we had Christmas morning—a body that resembled an older version of me.

"I know it's a long shot, but do you think we should pull the file on the couple they found on Reichl's property a few months back?" I asked Jake.

"You have a death wish? Garrett goes ape-shit if anyone touches one of his cases."

"I know but we've done everything else we can do until the DNA comes in, and even then we can't be sure it will tell us anything."

"I guess we don't have anything to lose."

Garrett and DiNucci were notorious for keeping most of the information from their investigations in paper files, so I searched the cabinets for the case. When I couldn't find it, I scoured Garrett's desk as Jake kept a lookout. The office was mostly empty, but neither of us wanted to risk getting caught rifling another detective's desk.

"Here it is," I said as I pulled the file from a stack of folders and papers.

We spread the file out on my desktop. It didn't look like our colleagues had done much to advance the investigation of the two victims, one male and the other female, both relatively young. No identification on either body. I flipped through pages to get to what I really wanted to see—autopsy photos.

They were at the back of the file—a white man with dark hair and full, jowly cheeks and a light-skinned black woman with close-cropped hair. Jake's eyes widened as he looked at the victims, each wearing a uniform with an insignia like our victim's. These two had been shot, a single bullet in the middle of the forehead.

"What the hell is going on?" I said.

As we both puzzled over the file, Doc walked into the office.

"You know anything about this?" Jake asked, showing her the photos of the murdered couple. "And this uniform."

Doc studied the photos and then checked the date on the police report. "This happened when I was out of town and Dillon did the autopsies. I never saw these."

Until Christmas morning, none of us had seen an insignia like this. Now we had three and damn, it also meant we'd have to work with Garrett and DiNucci.

"You have anything for us on our victim?" I asked.

"Well, we got an ID on the skin under the fingernail," she said.

"And?"

"And the DNA belongs to a man named Jeffrey Reichl."

"You mean Reichl as in Reichl Inc?" Jake asked.

"I don't know about the Inc part, but we traced his DNA through some old military records," Doc replied.

Jake and I both looked surprised and confused as Doc continued, "He served in the first Gulf War and is in his mid-40s today. He left the military not long after the war ended and last address we have is in Carmel."

"And what about the woman?" I asked.

Doc shook her head. "There was some kind of mix up in the lab and I had them redo the tests. I put a rush on it so we should have them back tomorrow."

Even if we didn't know the victim at least we had a suspect.

We checked both the Reichl business and his residence in Carmel and were told that he was out of the country and wouldn't return until next week. I didn't believe it. Jeffrey Reichl had to be in town and I hoped I could catch him off guard.

Jake and I took turns watching his home but didn't see anything until an afternoon four days after Christmas. I had parked outside his house when a limousine turned into the driveway, stopped in front of the house, and dropped off a man who went inside.

After the limo pulled away I rang the doorbell and after a moment it opened. Before me stood a man, slightly taller than me with a shock of white hair and deep blue eyes.

"Detective McGraw, I've been expecting you. Come in," he said.

"I'm here to see Jeffrey Reichl," I said, trying to sound confident even though I was unnerved by how this man seemed to know me.

"I'm Jeffrey Reichl," he replied.

"Then maybe it's your son *I'm* looking for," I said as I studied his face, covered with brown age spots and carved by deep lines around his eyes and mouth.

"I don't have a son. I'm the Jeffrey Reichl you're looking for," he said as he swung the door open wide and ushered me in.

This was the man I was looking for? Damn, he must have done a lot of hard living since the Gulf War because he looked at least twenty, maybe thirty years older than what I expected.

I couldn't tell whether he was smiling or smirking as he escorted me into a sitting room that would have held my entire apartment. A Christmas tree decorated in nothing but silver and twinkling white lights stood at least ten feet tall in the window while the opposite wall held three large-screen television sets. A faint scent of pine lingered in the room.

"I develop video games. That's my creative space," he said as my eyes were drawn to the wall of screens. "In fact, I like all kinds of games. Playing them. Developing them. Using them."

He directed me to sit in one of two Queen Anne chairs by the tree as he picked up a decanter of red wine and two glasses. He poured before I had a chance to tell him no, I was on duty.

"You must try this cabernet. It's from my vineyard in China."

Vineyard in China? I muttered no thanks even as he handed me the glass. I set it on the table between us.

"Try it. It's much smoother than the cheap wine you drink." His voice was low and rich, almost melodic.

I wanted to ask him how he knew what I drank, but I held my tongue.

"Mr. Reichl," I began.

"Jeffrey."

"Mr. Reichl, I need to know where you were at 2:48 a.m. Christmas morning."

"Eastern time?"

"Yes, sir. Eastern time."

"Let's see. Five-hour time difference between here and Lausanne and yes, I was having Christmas brunch with some friends in my hotel suite overlooking Lake Leman." He used the French name for Lake Geneva.

"I'll need some proof."

"Of course. Why don't you contact my friends directly. They're still in Switzerland. It's the Lausanne Palace." He checked his watch. "They're still up."

We had already confirmed with Homeland Security that his passport showed him leaving the United States on December 20 with no return. The question was how did he get back here Christmas morning to murder our victim.

"May I ask what this is about?" He studied me, his eyes moving from my face to my feet and before I could reply, he added, almost wistfully, "I forgot how lovely you were...are, even with your hair pulled back like that and those unflattering clothes."

"Look, I don't know what your game is, but this is about her. I want to know if you know this woman." I shoved the picture of our victim at him.

Reichl coolly studied the photo. "Hmmm. She doesn't look..." he paused, as if searching for the right word. "Alive. She doesn't look alive."

"She's not. She was murdered Christmas morning."

"Nasty wound." Reichl lightly touched his own neck.

"Mr. Reichl, we found your DNA under her fingernails," I said bluntly.

"How careless of me." He could have been talking about spilling a drop of his precious wine. He flexed his hands before lifting his glass. "You really should try this. I know how much you'll like it."

This was surreal. Did this man practically confess to murder? From the moment I entered this place Jeffrey Reichl acted like he knew me. I reflexively reached for my glass and took one large swallow.

"Slowly. You need to savor it," he said.

It dawned on me this was a game to him, but I wasn't sure what kind. I laid photos of the other two victims on the table in front of him.

"What about these two? You recognize them?"

"Hmmm. Same uniform. Interesting logo."

"Their bodies were dumped on your property on the west side about six months ago."

"I really must do something about security." He sounded bored.

"Mr. Reichl, maybe we should have this conversation downtown," I said, my hand on my weapon as I rose.

"That, my dear, will be a waste of your time and mine. My alibi is foolproof, absolutely foolproof."

Before I could respond, my phone buzzed. A text. I read it, and then read it again as I dropped into the chair.

"Is everything OK?" Reichl asked.

"Some puzzling information." I'm sure I looked as confused as I felt.

A knowing grin spread across Reichl's face. "It's the DNA, isn't it?"

"It's not about you," I said.

"No, not me," he said, no longer sounding bored. "It's that unfortunate woman, isn't it? And you."

"What?"

"The DNA." He paused. "The DNA has identified that poor, dead woman as Anne McGraw. You. I'm right, aren't I."

How did he know? Doc had texted me that the DNA tests were a mess because the results said the dead woman and I were the same person. Impossible.

"What are you up to, Mr. Reichl?" I demanded. I had planned to catch him off-guard with this visit and yet I was the one reeling. Nothing made sense. Reichl coolly swirled the wine in his glass.

"You act like you know me, yet we've never met," I said. "You practically admit to killing that woman and still you sit here chatting like we're old friends. Answer me. Do you know this woman?"

"What do you want me to say? That she and I had been very close...once?"

"So you *do* know who she is." I was regretting that I came here on my own and was thinking about how I should simply arrest him.

"Yes, Anne, you and I have had..." Reichl stopped. "Pardon me. You and I *will* have a long and stimulating relationship. At least for awhile."

"What the hell are you talking about?" I felt like I had walked into the third act of a Tennessee Williams play. Maybe I shouldn't have drunk that wine.

Reichl rose and strolled toward the bookcases. "You surprise me, Anne. I thought you would have figured it out by now. The uniforms, the insignia. Those bodies. What if I told you neither one of them has been born...yet."

"You're crazy." They had to be born before they could die. "Then how do you explain this?" I shoved the photos of the dead couple at him.

"I don't need to. You see, that's the genius of what I do. The problems of the future disposed of in the past, like these annoying police officers," he said, waving his hand at the photo.

Police officers? All three victims were police officers?

"And me, was I one of those future problems?" My head was spinning.

"Not always. You've been a challenge, but the game we were playing began to bore me so I decided to change it up," Reichl said, pushing against one of the bookcases to reveal a room on the other side.

As he stepped through the doorway, I drew my gun and commanded him to stop.

"You won't shoot," he said.

"Jeffrey Reichl, you're under arrest for the murder of..." I started to say.

"For what? The murder of you? Those two poor bastards?"

He was right. I would be laughed out of the department if I tried to charge him with murder considering his Christmas morning alibi and no way to connect him to the bodies on his property.

"Why are you telling me all this? Some kind of sick game?"

"Not a game," Reichl said, then stopped. "Not entirely a game. It's a business and a very lucrative one. People are willing to pay a princely sum to deposit the refuse of their world in the past. And *this* past, with its guns and violence, is perfect."

I raised my weapon and aimed at his midsection. "I can stop this right now."

"Don't be melodramatic." He extended his hand to me as he took a step into through the doorway. "Anne McGraw, I am giving you the chance to change your future. Come with me. Join me in this grand venture."

I lowered my gun, physically recoiling from this monster. "Grand venture? You murder people. I'm no murderer."

"Yet," he replied with a certainty that cut through me. I hesitated and in that split second Reichl turned and slipped through the doorway.

I darted across the room to stop him, but he was beyond my reach. I charged through the opening to find myself in a room the size of a closet. Reichl had vanished, but he left his business card lying on the floor:

Reichl Inc: Bury your troubles yesterday.

I picked it up, studying it as I considered my next step. I knew there was little I could do here and now, but I had thirty years to figure it out, thirty years to stop a killer…my killer.

Bloody Good Christmas Cookies

2 1/4 cups all-purpose flour

1 teaspoon baking powder

1 teaspoon baking soda

1 tablespoon corn starch

1 teaspoon salt

2 sticks unsalted butter, softened

2 large eggs

1 teaspoon vanilla extract

2 cups white chocolate chips

1 to 2 tubes of red food gel

Preheat oven to 350°F. In bowl, sift together flour, baking powder, baking soda, cornstarch, and salt. Set aside.

In a separate bowl, combine at medium speed the butter, eggs, and vanilla. Add the dry ingredients to the wet ingredients and mix (low speed is recommended) until dough is combined but not whipped. Scrape dough from sides of bowl to make sure all ingredients are combined.

Add white chocolate chips to the dough and mix at low speed.

Line a baking tray with parchment paper. Scoop 1/8 to 1/4 cup of cookie dough onto prepared tray.

For the bloody effect:

Take the tip of a tube of the gel and insert it into a cookie. Gently squeeze a small amount of the gel into the cookie. Repeat 2 to 3 times into each cookie.

Bake for 8 to10 minutes, rotating mid-way through the cycle to assure an even bake.

Let cool and you should have nice, blood-drippy white chocolate chip cookies.

— *Recipe courtesy of Sarah McKenzie*

The Reindeer Murder Case

By J. Paul Burroughs

I'd hoped to have a night on the town in Indianapolis with my best girl, Maisie, but instead, I found myself up to my elbows in a murder case.

My name's Mahoney. Nick Mahoney. I was born on Christmas Eve, so my mother named me after the blessed St. Nick. However, the good father at St. Anthony's used to remind me that "Ole Nick" referred to the devil. I guess there's more to me of the latter than the former.

I'm a gumshoe, a private investigator. I used to be a flatfoot cop in Indy before Uncle Sammy put me into a uniform and sent me out to the South Pacific to fight the Japs. I did pretty good out there until I took some shrapnel in my leg at Guadalcanal and after some time in a military hospital eventually was sent home.

I was tired of wearing a uniform, so I became a shamus. Good money for checking on cheating husbands, no good skirt-chasers and the like. No more dealing with dead bodies. Or so I thought.

This was my first Christmas back from the war. It was December, 1947, and I wanted to treat my girl, Maisie, to a show and a movie. I was game for any entertainment that did not include Hope, Crosby or (forgive me, gorgeous) Betty Grable. I'd read in *The Times* that there was a bunch of dolls who called themselves,

"The Rein-*dear-ies*," who performed on stage in a show the news-paper columnist said, "shouldn't be missed." I'd heard from a buddy also back from the war that these babes had gams a preacher's kid could kill over.

My buddy was right. These ladies, dressed in reindeer antlers, bells, skimpy red and green skirts and sheer nylon stockings, knew how to strut their stuff. When they finished their first number, the audience went nuts with applause.

When their act was over, the theater showed a short on some island paradise. I stepped out to use the john and have a smoke when that came on. I'd had enough of South Pacific islands to last me for the rest of my life.

When I returned, the movie had already started. Jimmy Stew-art was asking Donna Reed to dance with him in the school gym-nasium. My keister was barely in the seat, when a terrible scream came from the backstage. It was followed by more screams.

I leaned into Maisie. "Don't go nowhere, gorgeous." I got up to see what was going on.

I knew the theater. When I was a smart mouth kid, I used to slip inside the back door to the place to catch Boris prowling about on screen as Frankenstein or Lugosi vamping the ladies in Dracula. When I got a little older, I'd take a peek at the dancers changing after a show. But that's another story.

I reached the dressing room and found the Rein-dearies peer-ing inside a storage closet where a body lay on the floor. I could tell in a moment that the body was part of their troupe by the antlers and bright skirt.

"It's Lucy," one of the girls sobbed. "We knew she probably ran late—too late to make the show, but we never thought we'd find her dead."

I bent down to look at the body. Even in death, this one was a looker, despite the nylon stocking wrapped tightly around her neck.

Strangled. Tough way to go.

"Step back! Step back, alla ya!" a voice called out from the door to the dressing room. I recognized it immediately. The girls parted like the Red Sea, and Detective Danny Sullivan stepped into my sight. He looked down at me bending over the corpse and shook his head.

"Mahoney, what the hell are you doing here?"

Danny and I did our basic training together. However, he ended up in the European theatre, and I ended up in the Pacific. The war had aged him. Although we both were twenty-eight, he looked like a man in his forties.

"I came for the show, but stayed for the murder," I replied.

He turned to the dancers. "Can any of you give me a name for this broad?"

"I can." A short guy in glad rags shuffled over to join us, a stogie in his hand. "Her name's Lucille, Lucille Greenstreet."

"But we all called her Lucy," a cute broad with eyes like twin topazes spoke up.

"And whose little girl might you be?"

"My name's Beverly, if you hafta know."

Danny turned to the guy who'd give him the corpse's name. "And you, Mister?"

"I'm the manager for these girls. You got questions, Flatfoot? I'm the man to see."

Danny bristled over being called a flatfoot. "And my name's Sullivan—Detective Daniel O'Shaughnessy Sullivan. But you can call me 'Sir.' What can you tell me about this doll?"

"She's dead."

"Smart guy, eh? What else can you tell me?"

"She auditioned for my troupe two months ago. She was a looker, could dance well, and could do what she was told, so I hired her."

"Define, 'do what she was told,'" Danny insisted.

"Some of my girls—they have problems with the dance routines. When I see that, I have them stay after rehearsal for some *extra* practice."

"Yeah, practice in the horizontal position," quipped one of the dancers.

"Shut yer face!"

"We shoulda known something was wrong," Beverly again spoke up.

"Why is that?"

"It ain't normal for her to be late. She has…*had*…this thing about getting places early. Until now, she was never late showing up here."

"Looks to me," I added my two cents, "that she got here early after all. Someone wasted her and hid the body."

"Who found her this way?" Danny asked.

One of the dames raised a hand. "I did."

"And your name?"

"Arlene. When we finished our act and came back here, I noticed the door was open a crack. Normally it's kept locked. I looked inside and found her."

"Anyone here knows where this Lucy was living?"

A knock-your-socks-off beautiful redhead spoke up. "I do. She shares a flat with me."

"And you would be?"

"Rosaline Lamour."

"That your real name or your stage one?"

This time a doll with hair as black as coal spoke up. "Her real name is Myrtle—Myrtle Corcoran."

"Myrtle, can you give me your address?"

The dame shot the other dancer a look that could freeze boiling water. She gave an address on East Washington Street. I took out a pad and wrote it down for further reference. Danny told her he'd stop by the following day and look through the dead doll's things. Although I didn't say it, I decided I'd drop in, as well.

"I'd like to speak with each one of you in private before you leave the theater," Danny told the dancers.

A buxom blonde eased herself closer to him. "If you like, you can question me at my place. I'll do anything you want to cooperate, Detective."

He cleared his throat and tugged at his collar. "I'll question you all here, if you don't mind. Mahoney, you want in on this? We used to work pretty well together. And to be honest, half of homicide is down with some sort of cold that's goin' around."

I knew Maisie was probably boiling that I wasn't watching the picture beside her. I could hear Jimmy Stewart talking to some old coot who was insisting that he was an angel. Still, I already had one foot into this case, and decided I'd add the other foot as well.

"Count me in..." I started to say Danny but changed my mind. "...Detective."

The theatre manager agreed to give up his office for Danny's interrogation.

꙳ꙮ꙳ ꙮ꙳ꙮ ꙳ꙮ꙳

"Your name?" he asked the first dancer. She was a brunette, possibly the tallest of all the girls. She had eyes like Lauren Bacall and legs like Ann Miller.

"Lana DuVal."

"That your stage name?" I asked.

"That's my real name, Sugar."

"How well did you know the deceased?"

"A little. After the show, we sometimes go down to a bar on Illinois Street for a beer. Give a gal a Pabst and she'll spill about things."

"What sort of *things?*"

"Where she came from, the family back home."

"Where was home?"

"She grew up in Kokomo. She got out of high school there and signed on with the USO in forty-four. Was a dancer to entertain the GI's over in Europe. She had a boyfriend who was in the army."

"Where's this boyfriend now?"

"He died in France. Took a bullet, or so she said."

"Any new men in her life?"

"Some stage-door Johnny's come by a few times and left her flowers. I think she turned him down, when he asked her out, though."

We talked some more, and I noticed a bright green choker on her neck with the single name, Blixen.

"Did all the dancers wear chockers with reindeer names on them?"

She told me they did. I thought about the dead girl. What name had she been given? The only thing I'd seen around her neck was the stocking that had killed her.

While Danny interrogated the redhead, I slipped out and asked the sleezeball manager.

"Her? Lemme see. Yeah, she was Vixen."

I wondered if it was just the name she'd been given for the shows, or whether she'd tried to live up to the name, and that was what made someone want to off her.

When I got back to where Danny was holding interrogations, the redhead was in there. The choker around her neck identified her as Dancer. Danny asked her the same questions he'd asked the blonde, but Myrtle was more defensive.

"How should I know who she seeing? I ain't her social secretary," she said.

"You two shared a flat," he reminded her. "Shouldn't you know if some bozo had a thing for Lucy?"

"I got my own self to look out for." Myrtle fell silent for a few moments. Then, "Yeah, come to think of it, some Romeo dropped by as I was going out the door one afternoon. I could tell Lucy knew the guy from before. He mentioned a message he was to give her from her folks back from wherever she came from."

"Kokomo," I prompted.

"Yeah…whatever."

"Did you catch this rube's name?" Danny asked.

"Like I said. I wasn't her social secretary. She said it, but I can't remember it."

"Do you recall what he looked like, then?"

"He was short. I remember that. Had red hair—darker than mine. Freckles, too. I know—he looked like that kid in some comic books—the one who hangs around with the chump in the pointy hat. He was young—probably a coupla years younger than Lucy. There've been a few nights lately when she was gone for hours after the show, showing up at three in the morning. Didn't tell me if she was out with a fella or simply grabbing drinks at some bar. That's all I know."

The other members of the dance troupe had nothing more to add. While we'd been talking with the ladies, the meat wagon pulled up at the stage door and took away the body. I arranged to meet with Danny tomorrow at the address he'd been given for the dead dame.

When I returned to Maisie, on screen a little girl was looking up at Jimmy Stewart and telling him some story about a bell and an angel getting wings. I'd missed almost all the movie. Maisie blew her stack. She told me to take a hike. She was going home in a taxi. She told me to give the taxi driver a fiver, and the taxi shot off down Illinois Street like the devil was after it. I went back to where I'd parked my 1941 Studebaker and drove home. I'd blown my big night out with Maisie.

At nine the next morning, I met Danny at a three-story apartment building on East Washington Street. Lucy and Myrtle had a flat on the third floor. We trudged up the two flights of stairs amid noise of a baby screaming its guts out, and someone on the second floor listening to a Benny Goodman record.

We found the room and Danny knocked. There was no sound from inside. He knocked again, this time calling out, "Miss Corcoran, this is the police. Open up."

Still no response.

He knocked a third time. He knocked the door so hard, it was a wonder his hand didn't go through the wood. This time, I could hear someone moving about. The door handle turned. I could barely make out Myrtle behind a small chain.

"What do you want? Do you know what time it is?"

Danny checked his watch. "Nine fifteen." He flashed his badge. "Remember me? Detective Sullivan? You agreed to let me look through Lucy's belongings?"

She grumbled some things that if my mother was to read this, I'd be in deep trouble. So, I won't quote her word for word. Let's just say she wasn't happy. She took off the chain and let us in.

One look at her that morning could make someone believe in the whole Jekyll and Hyde story. Her hair was a mess, her nightgown wrinkled, and her face—well, it definitely needed makeup. Judging by the empty bottle of gin on the table, she'd had a snootful after leaving us at the theater.

"Where are Lucy's things?" Danny asked.

She made a motion with one hand directing us to a bed, a suitcase, and a chest of drawers.

"Anything else?"

She gave a flick of a hand in the direction of a closet.

Danny searched the chest of drawers, and I took the closet.

I found a couple of day dresses, a robe, and two gowns that she probably used for hitting nightspots whenever a guy talked her into going out. Two pair of shoes were strategically placed in the front of the closet.

"Hey, come and look at these," Danny called out to me. He'd opened a drawer and had laid out some of her undergarments. Under them, he'd found some cards like the kind you send with flowers. "Take a gander at these—especially the last one."

One was from a guy named Johnny. No last name.

Two more wished her love from a guy named Arch. For some reason, I suspected he was the red-haired kid, Myrtle had told us about. I looked at the last card and felt like Columbus when he first got an eyeful of America.

Love and kisses doll,

Chester T.

I didn't need to check the phone directly to identify what the T stood for.

Chester Thornton, aka "Gunsel" Thornton.

Danny and I exchanged a look. Thornton came out of Chicago just prior to the war. He'd moved to Indianapolis and by 1942, had his finger in every bit of pie involving gambling, robbery, and when it was required, murder. However, the John Q. Public didn't know that. Even if they did, they ignored such talk. Thornton had poured big money in support of the war effort. At bond rallies, he was usually present dropping big bills into the war chest, getting his mug in the newspapers. But most people didn't know the man's festering underbelly.

He had an eye for beauty and was always seen in public with a gorgeous dame on his arm. As I looked down at the card, it was clear that on at least one occasion, Lucy Greenstreet had been on that arm.

After leaving Lucy's flat I drove over to the *The Indianapolis*

News building. I went up to an office on the third floor where "Gossip Gigi" worked. Her name is Gladys Graham. She's the society columnist for the paper. If something's going on with society's tops here in the city, Gladys knows about it.

She was munching on a sandwich from a downtown deli when I arrived on her doorstep. "Well, well, if it ain't the poor man's Sherlock Holmes," she greeted me. "What poor sucker did I screw around with to deserve you dropping by?"

"Good to see you, too, Gladys. You're lookin' well."

"So, 'I'm looking well,' is it? What do you need, Gumshoe?"

"Information. I need to know what you have on one Lucille Greenstreet and Chester Thornton."

"She the gal who got bumped off last night?"

I nodded.

"You back on the force again?"

I shook my head. "Just decided to give Detective Sullivan a hand. That's all. So, what do you have on her?"

"The past few weeks, Chester's been seen squiring her around town."

"Think she might have found out some things she shouldn't oughta?"

"Could have. Might not have. If you're looking for someone with a motive for killing her, you should check Arlene."

I started to ask who Arlene was, and then remembered one of the dancers we'd spoken to last night. Arlene was the reindeer Donner in the production.

"Why would she want to kill Lucy?"

"I told you, your victim was cozying up with Thornton, right? Three guesses who was Chester's girl before Lucy?"

"Arlene?"

"Hit the nail right on the head. Understand Arlene raised holy Ned when Thornton dropped her for Lucille. My source said she threatened to kill her."

"Thanks, Gladys. You're all right."

"Tell that to my ex-husband."

෴ ෴ ෴

I found a phone booth and arranged to meet Danny at a dive off Georgia Street. I wanted to fill him in on what I'd just learned. We found a booth, and I spilled my guts. Strangely enough, he wasn't impressed.

"You got it all wrong, Mahoney. The member of the dance troupe who wanted her dead wasn't Arlene."

"Why do you say that?"

"It was that broad with the farm girl expression for a face."

I thought back. "Judy?"

"That's the one."

I remembered her. She was the Dasher reindeer in the dance number. She'd told us, her folks worked a farm over in nearby Hancock County.

"What motive would that sweet lookin' broad have for wanting to kill Lucy?"

"Remember the GI boyfriend who died in France? Judy's his kid sister. I learned that not long before he got burned by a Kraut, he received a 'Dear John' letter from Lucy. He died a day later. Just left cover and ran straight at a machine gun nest not caring whether he lived or died. My snitch said Judy blamed our corpse for his death."

"You gonna haul her in?"

"Not yet. Got another lead. A bartender at a joint where the dancers often visited after the show told me to speak to some palooka named Angelo Rossi. Seems he's cozy with Beverly, the one who told us Myrtle's real name."

I remembered her—the one with jet black hair. "Got an address?"

He nodded.

"Can I come along?"

"Thought you'd never ask."

~:~ ~:~ ~:~

Beverly, last name Manelli, was the show's Comet reindeer. An Italian. The same went for her boyfriend, Angelo Rossi. We tracked him to a single-story double on East Michigan Street.

"You looking for who bumped off the Greenstreet dame?"

"We are. A bartender we talked to said you might have information to help us."

He held out an open palm. "What's in it for me?"

Danny was all for smacking the guy around to get the information. I stopped him and laid a five spot in his open palm.

He rolled his eyes at the five and kept his palm out. "I'm having memory problems. It'll get better if you double that."

I stepped back and waved a hand in Rossi's direction to let Danny go ahead with his original intentions. Rossi saw what he was about to get pummeled and cracked.

"Okay, you don't gotta make a punching bag outa me. I'll talk."

He pointed out that there was an even better candidate for the murderer than either Arlene or Judy. Beverly had told him that Laverne, the sandy haired dancer who wore a choker with the name Rudolph had a grudge against our victim.

"This Lucy dame was in a jam and needed some money. Laverne loaned her a twenty. A week later, Lucy paid her back. When Laverne went to buy some groceries, she learned the bill was queer—a counterfeit. Laverne came this close to getting busted. When she confronted Lucy, that dame swore on a Bible that she didn't know it was fake. Laverne told my girl, that she was certain the dame was lying. Told her that one day, she'd get even. Guess that day was last night."

Danny wanted to make Rossi give me my fiver back, but I said that the information he'd given us was genuine. I told Rossi to keep the dough, and we left.

You know how you sometimes get a feeling about something? I got that feeling about the roommate, Rosaline, alias Myrtle, alias Dancer. I remembered the flat she shared with Lucy had paper thin walls. I figured that if they didn't get along, the person in the flat next door might know.

After Danny and I split up, I drove back to the apartment building. I knocked on the door of the apartment next to theirs and waited. A woman answered the door.

"Whatever you're selling, I ain't buying." She tried to slam the door in my face.

My foot was faster and kept the door open. I asked her if there had been any trouble between the two dames.

"Trouble? When *ain't* there been trouble between those two? They start yelling from the time they go through the doorway. Sometimes they go at until three in the morning. I work at a factory and need my sleep. Do they care? Not likely. I've complained to the landlord, but I figure he's got the hots for the one still alive."

"Do you think Myrtle hated Lucy enough to kill her?" I asked.

"So, that's her name? Yeah, I think so."

I left the apartment building with another name to add to our list of probable murderers.

When we'd split up, Danny had told me he was going to try and find out about the cute blonde who had put the make on him the night before. Her reindeer name was Prancer. I wondered if he planned to talk to her at her place, do some "sky-watching" and possibly get lucky. When I told him what I thought he was up to, he laughed in my face.

"In no way am I going to get alone with that one. I hear she works part time at a restaurant on the Westside. I plan on talking with someone who waits tables with her."

My phone was ringing when I got to my office. It was Danny. He'd learned nothing that would make the blonde a suspect. He said he was calling it quits.

I was about to do the same when an idea hit me. I drove down to the morgue hoping I'd find the coroner. I lucked out. He was just ready to leave for the day when I got there.

"You have the stockings that were used to strangle the dancer, right?"

"I was about to hand it over for storage in the evidence locker."

"These stockings—they come in different sizes, right?"

"Yeah."

I had an idea. Thought I'd play the whole Prince Charming-Cinderella gambit. The thought of personally trying the nylons on each off the dancers sounded very appealing, if you catch my drift.

But Doc shot me down.

"Won't work. The nylons are brand new. Don't look like they've ever been worn. The killer just bought the first pair he or she saw," he told me.

Suddenly, I got a better idea.

⛌ ⛌ ⛌

The following evening, I showed up at Maisie's flat. I'd brought a box of chocolates, a bouquet, and a box of nylons. I already *knew* Maisie's size. She met me at the door, but wasn't ready to forgive me and let me in. "So, you think this will make me forgive you for being such a louse the other night?"

"I'll never do it again, I swear it."

She looked me up and down trying to decide if I was worth another chance.

"That's a new tie. I never saw that before."

"I bought it to celebrate."

She raised an eyebrow. "To celebrate what?"

"Breaking the case. I caught the murderer."

She looked doubtful but let me in. Over a beer, I told her about all that had led up to my solving the murder.

"So, the coroner told you the stockings were new…"

"Yeah, and then it hit me. Although they didn't look all that expensive, I decided to hit some of the better stores in Indianapolis. I made the rounds of Blocks, Penneys, and L. S. Ayres. I struck pay dirt at Ayres. The brand used for the murder was only sold there."

"So, the clerk who sold the stockings knew who bought them?"

I shook my head. "No, she sells a decent amount now that the war's over, and the restrictions have been lifted."

"Well, how did knowing where the stockings came from help?"

"Before I answer you, I need you to answer a question I've got."

"Okay, shoot."

"You go downtown and buy something at a department store. You pay and the clerk hands you the receipt. What do you do with it?"

"Stick it in my purse. Why?"

"I talked things over with Danny, and he got a search warrant to go through the dancer's things while they were out on stage performing—especially purses. In one, we found a receipt for the stockings balled up. We went through the doll's apartment and found the other stocking stuffed in the trash bin behind her building. I told you those dancers were gorgeous, not smart. We confronted the dame and under pressure, she confessed."

"Well, don't keep me in suspense. Who killed the girl?"

"I'll tell you, if you agree to go dancing with me tonight."

"Okay, you got me on a string. Who done it?"

I grinned. It seems Arlene was more than just a little peeved about losing Chester, her "million bucks" meal ticket, to Lucy. I thought about the reindeer name on the choker around Arlene's own neck as she strangled her victim.

I also thought about those lines you see in Christmas cards. As I'd driven over to Maisie's I made up a jingle of my own to answer her.

Comet's a cutie,
But she didn't off Vixen.
Dasher's in the clear,
And so is Miss Blixen.
It's Donner who done it,
Not Dasher or Prancer,
Let's go hit the ballroom.
You're my favorite Dancer.

I danced the night away with Maisie.

Christmas Reindeer Roast

2 tablespoons plus 1/2 tablespoon cooking oil

3 to 4 pounds venison roast (beef may be substituted)

1/4 cup onion, chopped

1 tablespoon garlic, minced

1 cup carrots, sliced

3 cups low sodium beef broth

1/4 cup red wine (Lumbrusco preferred)

2 (10 3/4-ounce) cans of cream of mushroom soup

1 teaspoon salt

1 cup canned sliced mushrooms

In a skillet add 1/2 tablespoon of the cooking oil and brown each side of the roast.

Add remaining cooking oil to the bottom of a pressure cooker. Add onions, garlic and carrots. Cook the vegetables at medium heat for 3 to 4 minutes or until softened.

Add beef broth, wine and soup, stirring repeatedly until the mixture is smooth.

Add the roast. Season with salt. Then add mushrooms.

Cover the pressure cooker and set burner on medium heat and cook for 50 minutes.

Add a cup of water at that time and continue to cook for 30 more minutes or until tender.

Serve with mashed potatoes, or white rice.

Claus, Santa: MIA

By C. L. Shore

ava was up before dawn the morning of December twenty-fourth. Thankfully, she'd wrapped her gifts earlier in the month. The L. S. Ayres' employee discount made her Christmas shopping extremely easy and somewhat economical. She'd even had enough money left over to buy herself two sweater twinsets, one in cardinal red and one in evergreen. A small balsam fir occupied the corner of her tiny apartment, decorated with red velvet bows.

Mava savored the feeling of safety during the holidays. Last year, she'd been in Europe, nursing wounded GIs. Many of them were her age, some even younger. Now, she was back on American soil, and so were some of her patients—those who survived.

Janet, her coworker, grumbled about having to work the day before Christmas, but Mava welcomed the opportunity to put in her shift in Appliances and Housewares. She'd had enough of nursing for a while and found it a welcome change to work in a place where chaos didn't reign, where wounded weren't carried in at all hours of the day and night, and where there was a definite quitting time. And no blood involved. She made enough money to pay the rent on her St. Claire Street apartment just north of downtown Indianapolis. She could walk to work, go to church on Monument Circle on Sundays and take the Interurban to visit her folks and kid brother in Plainfield on her days off. Some of the others in her

Army Nurse Corps squadron might call her life boring. The routine and dependability agreed with Mava, though. She could live a boring life for the time being.

The atmosphere at Ayres transitioned from pleasant to festive when the Santa Cottage opened. The little house with gingerbread shutters occupied a space just around the corner from Housewares. Even though Mava couldn't see the cottage itself from her cash register, she could see the line of children as they eagerly awaited their turn to sit on Santa's lap. Sometimes they came to her department with their mothers after their experience, wide-eyed and clutching candy canes.

Just the day before, the red-suited gentleman had wandered into Housewares. He'd approached Mava. "Have you been good all year, young lady?" he'd asked.

"I've tried to be," Mava replied. Santa's voice sounded awfully young to her. "You could ask my supervisor, Mrs. Baker. I haven't missed a day of work. Of course, I just hired on three months ago."

"Hmm." Santa nodded. He stood in front of Mava and pulled on the fluffy white beard to reveal his features, including a pair of hazel eyes protected by auburn brows. His was a youthful face. Mava guessed this jolly old elf couldn't be out of his twenties.

"Name's Nick," he said. "Really. I think my moniker helped me get the job."

Mava smiled. "I'm Mava, named after my grandmother. Don't know if my name helped me get this job or not."

Nick returned her smile. "Nice to meet you, Mava. Maybe we can get together after the holiday. I might be working in the luggage department then. In civilian garb." He waved a mittened hand and started toward the elevator.

"I hope so." Mava called after him. Maybe her comment sounded rather forward, but she didn't care. The war had emphasized just how precious life was. She didn't believe in wasting a minute of it.

Janet's blond hair was visible across two aisles of pots and pans.

She'd witnessed the entire exchange and crossed over to the cash register on tiptoe.

"I think Santa likes you," she said in a stage whisper.

Mava shrugged. "Maybe." They both giggled.

It seemed reasonable to expect exchanging a "Merry Christmas" with Santa himself on that December twenty-fourth. Endless rows of excited boys and girls would wind through the aisle of kitchen gadgets, each awaiting their turn on Santa's lap.

Children and parents crowded along the downtown sidewalk, waiting to burst through the department store doors at nine o'clock. Young and old alike directed their attention to the windows with their detailed display of skating and sledding scenes. Machines hidden from view kept the skaters circling the lake and the sleds hurtling down the hillside.

Mava scurried through the employee's entrance, hung her coat and purse in her locker, and took the elevator to the eighth floor. Instead of animated conversation and cheerful faces, she found several somber employees affixing a poster to the front of Santa's Cottage. "Santa is busy making toys today," it read. "Sorry he can't be here."

Mava grabbed the elbow of one of the maintenance workers and gestured toward the sign. "What's going on?" she demanded. "I saw Nick yesterday. I'm sure he was planning to be here."

"You haven't seen the papers, have you, lady?" the man said. He grabbed a rolled-up piece of newsprint from under his tool box and folded it to reveal the front page.

Mava's hand flew to her mouth when she saw the headline: *Is Santa Dead?* She hurriedly skimmed the columns of print. A red Santa suit was found on Washington Street, about five blocks east of the department store. Red stains, thought to be blood, were found on the white wool down the front of the jacket. Although Santa himself was not located, the local police suspected a crime had been committed. Possibly homicide.

Homicide. Did Nick meet with foul play? Mava felt sick at the thought. And sad. How could this be happening? She'd lost friends and patients so many times during the war. Nick wasn't exactly a friend yet, but she'd hoped that he would be.

Concentrating during her busy shift proved difficult. There were multitudes of shoppers, many accompanied by children. Mava heard one boy of about ten say to his younger sister, "Do you think Santa will come this year? Maybe there won't be any Christmas." The younger girl's eyes welled with tears and she stifled a sob. Her mother grabbed her daughter in a bear hug. "You hush your mouth, now," she said to the boy. Harsh words, but her tone was gentle. "Of course, there will be Christmas this year. Don't worry," she said to both children in a soothing tone.

Mava wished she could be reassured. Janet didn't say a word about Nick, but she did give her a quick hug before leaving. "Merry Christmas," she said. "Everything will be fine. You'll see."

Mava clocked out and walked home in gently falling snow. Ordinarily, she'd be enchanted with the snowflakes and their arrival on Christmas Eve. Tonight, though, she only wanted to get home and lock the door behind her. Once in her apartment, she forced herself to place her wrapped presents in a large Ayres shopping bag, so they'd be ready for the trip to Plainfield the next day. Her task finished, she curled up on the settee and stared out the window.

Mava arose Christmas morning with a hollow feeling in her chest. She dressed in her plaid skirt and the new bright red twinset, wishing she could feel more festive. After smoothing her dark brown hair, she added the holly barrette she'd bought on a whim at G. C. Murphy's five and dime. Her brother picked her up in his newly purchased sedan, so proud of his first car, even though it sported a few dents and a little rust. In his enthusiasm, he didn't notice her distraction. Once back at the family homestead, the gift exchange was lively and her mother's dinner excellent. But even her favorite anise cookies didn't brighten Mava's mood. She saw her father flash a glance of concern her way.

"We're so glad you're home this year," he said, giving her a little squeeze of a hug.

He probably thinks that I'm remembering incidents during the war. When twilight fell, Mava asked her brother to take her home.

December twenty-sixth was a chaotic churning of humanity at Ayres, everyone bringing in their yuletide gifts for exchange. During a brief break, Mava checked her company mailbox. A tiny notecard in an envelope lay on its shelf. The brief message inside was dated December twenty-third.

I was quite serious when I said I wanted to get to know you better. Looking forward to the New Year.

(St.) Nick.

Mava bit her lip.

At the close of her day, police detectives arrived in the housewares department. They explained their case was technically a missing person's case. There was no body, so they couldn't say that a murder had been committed. Still, the blood on the Santa Suit suggested someone had met with a violent encounter. And Nick was missing.

Everyone who worked on the eighth floor was asked to stay after hours. One at a time, they were ushered into the break room. When Mava entered, the detective asked her about her interactions with the department store Santa.

Mava had little to say. He intrigued her, she admitted. She was looking forward to getting to know him better. "But actually," she said. "I knew very little about him. He told me first name was Nick, but I didn't know his last name. He seemed to be a loyal employee, though, and his disappearance struck me as being out of character. He said he was going to work in the luggage department after the holidays."

She remembered the note. "I found this today."

The two detectives looked at it and handed it back to her. "It does look like he intended to return to work," the taller one said, shrugging his shoulders. "If you think of anything else, here's my card."

Mava put the card in her pocket. She tried to ask the detectives a few questions, but they were evasive. On her way out of the room, she saw a discarded newspaper in the wastebasket and picked it up. She could only bring herself to read one paragraph of the update on the Santa story. No body. No distinct footprints leaving the scene. The sidewalks surrounding the area where the suit was found were either bare, or a sloppy mess of boot tracks on top of each other. Sounded like the police had little information to work with.

Janet came out of the detectives' temporary office a few minutes later. She met Mava's eyes, her own expression somber. "Tell you what," her coworker said. "Let's grab a bite down the block at the hamburger counter. I could use someone to talk to before I go home tonight."

Mava locked arms with her. "Agreed. Let's get our coats and be on our way."

A few minutes later, they were looking out the diner's dark windows, watching passers-by. The wind was picking up, more than one gentleman lost his hat to a gust as he rounded the corner onto Washington Street.

"This whole thing is so sad." Janet sipped a cherry cola and munched on a hamburger. "I'm going to ask Skip what he knows about Nick." Mava knew Skip was a friend of Janet's brother and he worked in the furniture department.

Mava took a long draw of her 7 Up. "I'm going to talk to the Personnel Department. Don't know if they'll tell me, but I'm going to try and find out where Nick lived."

"Wasn't his address in the newspaper?"

Mava shook her head. "Don't know. I could only bring myself to skim the articles. But if Nick didn't live alone, and I can talk with whoever lived with him, maybe I could learn something useful. Even if he lived by himself, there might be a neighbor."

Janet cocked her head. "Your idea might pan out. I'll see if Skip knows anything about his address, too."

꒪꒪꒱ ꒪꒪꒱ ꒪꒪꒱

Mava could hardly wait to see Janet the next morning. She'd come in a few minutes early and stopped in Personnel. They wouldn't give her Nick's address, but they did share his last name: Mickleson. At least she had a full name to work with.

Janet seemed out of breath as she approached the cash register. "I don't have an address for Nick. At least, not yet. But I was just down on the seventh floor, visiting Skip. He told me that Nick lived with his brother Thomas."

"And I know their last name is Mickleson!" Mava realized she was almost shouting when two heads turned their way from across the aisle. She lowered her head and whispered. "With a first and last name to work with, I'm sure I can come up with something."

During her morning stop for coffee in the break room, Mava found the telephone book located under the phone provided for employees. A number and address were listed for Thomas Mickleson, but not for Nick. Thomas lived on Massachusetts Avenue, less than a mile from Ayres. Mava had the next day off because she'd worked Christmas Eve. She'd head over to the Mickleson address first thing in the morning.

꒪꒪꒱ ꒪꒪꒱ ꒪꒪꒱

Sunshine streamed through her bedroom window. Almost nine o'clock! Mava washed her face and dressed quickly. After a bite of toast, she bounded down the two flights of stairs from her apartment and emerged onto the sidewalks of St. Clair. The bright sun-shine helped to boost her mood. Maybe she'd find out something from Thomas. Hopefully, he'd be at home.

She arrived at the Massachusetts Avenue address in less than fifteen minutes. She entered the vestibule and scanned the mail-boxes. A thin placard under the box for apartment 303 bore the name "Mickleson". She walked up three flights of stairs and found the door for apartment 303 on the north side of the hallway. She inhaled sharply, then knocked as she let out a pent-up breath.

"Who's there?" The voice was masculine, sharp—almost hostile.

"I'm a friend of Nick's." Mava felt her heart rate accelerate. She never thought of telling anyone her plan for the day. She should have given Janet the specifics, at least.

The door opened abruptly, causing Mava to let out a little yelp. She found herself eyeball to eyeball with a man in a bathrobe, tat-tered corduroys peeking out from its hem. While Mava struggled to come up with something to say, the man's expression softened a little.

"I'm sorry, miss." He hung his head and sighed. "It's just that I've been wound tighter than a top since my brother disappeared. I hope you have some good news for me."

Mava took a deep breath. "I wish I did. But I thought if I had a chance to talk to you, his brother, maybe that could help find him. I just met Nick recently, so I really don't know much about him." The man looked at her with a blank expression. "I worked with Nick. I'm a sales clerk on the eighth floor, the same floor as the Santa Cottage."

The man nodded his head. "I'm Nick's brother, Thomas. But you probably already figured that out. Come in, come in."

Mava felt she could risk entering his apartment. *Really, I have no choice if I want to find Nick.* It appeared Thomas' unit only had windows facing the northwest, and the place seemed dark and dreary, even on this sunny day. Thomas indicated she could sit in an armchair, while he moved some newspapers and sat on a worn sofa. The room smelled of stale tobacco; an ashtray at Thomas's elbow was crowded with unfiltered butts.

"I was hoping to learn something that could help me find Nick," she began in a gentle voice. "I only met him the day before he disappeared, and he seemed so nice. Did he enjoy his position, playing Santa?"

Thomas put his face in his hands, then met Mava's gaze before answering. "He loved that job, sister. See, he was in the war, in Europe, as a medic. He saw some awful bad stuff there, would never talk about it much. He said this job was a chance to spread happiness for the season. After Christmas, he was planning on a place in the luggage department."

"Yes, Nick mentioned that," Mava nodded. "But I didn't know that he'd been a soldier. I'm a nurse and was in the ANC. Nick and I probably had some experiences that were similar."

"That may be true," Thomas nodded. "Do you have nightmares? There's been times that I heard Nick moan in his sleep."

"Yes, I understand about nightmares." Mava paused before asking another question. "Can you tell me a little about what Nick did when he wasn't at work?"

Thomas looked across the room before answering. "Well, he'd go for long walks. At least that's what he said. He said he found groups of homeless men, especially under the bridges, near the river. Some of them had been GIs. He said he felt sorry for them. After his shift, he'd buy up all the unsold pastries in the fancy cookie department and take a big box of them down to the men."

Mava managed a little smile. "Nick sounds like a sweet guy. Did you ever go with him on his walks?" Maybe she could find out specifics of his route.

Thomas gave her a quick, lopsided smile while he shook his head. "Naw, I couldn't keep up with him." He raised his corduroys to a couple inches below the knee. His right leg looked normal, but the left had a much thinner appearance, the calf muscle was underdeveloped.

"You had polio. I'm so sorry."

Thomas nodded. "Yep. I was 4-F. Walking more than a block is tough, especially at Nick's pace." He let his pantlegs fall to cover his legs.

Mava reached forward and put a hand on Thomas's knee. "It sounds like Nick has a concerned brother, one who's worried about him." She stood. "Thanks for sharing your information with me, I'm going to see if I can't use it to discover Nick's whereabouts."

"I'm wishing you all of the luck in the world, lady. Hope you find him."

"Thank you, Thomas. I'll let myself out."

Returning to the sidewalk with its bright sunshine and crisp shadow brightened Mava's mood just a smidgin. The situation about Nick was certainly bleak and sitting in the apartment he shared with Thomas only made it seem more so. She crossed her fingers. *Let me find Nick alive and well.* Surely, if he started regular employment in the luggage department, he'd be able to afford a better apartment.

She was touched by the story about the sweets. She could walk around the bridges near the White River and Fall Creek. Maybe she'd run into someone who'd know something. Any tidbit of information might help. She tried to think of bridges near the downtown area, places where Nick might walk after work or on his days off. There was a bridge near the City Hospital, one several blocks west of Ayres, and one north of the downtown area and not far from her own apartment. She'd try to get to them all today.

She walked across the downtown area and stopped in the diner she'd visited with Janet for a quick sandwich and a cup of coffee. After she finished her hurried meal, she put on the cap and gloves she'd wadded into her pocket, buttoned up her coat, and headed to the riverfront near the City Hospital. Once she'd half-slid, half sidestepped to the bank, she could see a few shacks made of scraps of wood. A few were constructed out of cardboard. Smoke rose from one of them. It was a wretched place and the genteel would have avoided setting foot near it. But she'd been in worse, with shells exploding all around.

A man wrapped in an army blanket approached her. His grizzled face could've been belonged to a man of twenty-five or forty-five years. She caught a glimpse of a metal chain against the back of his neck—probably attached to a dog tag.

"We don't see many ladies down around these parts." His voice was scratchy, tentative.

Mava felt a little shaky. "I expect you don't." She managed a smile. "Fact is, I was trying to find out something about a man named Nick. I heard he brought treats down to the river. Do you know him?"

The man shook his head and spat tobacco juice on the ground. "Nick!" he said, shaking his head. "I haven't seen him for a few days. Sure miss the cookies and doughnuts. And his terrible jokes."

Mava nodded. "It would help me a lot if you could tell me the last time you saw him. Can you think back? How many days has it been?"

The man looked down at the ground. Mava could see his fingers flex in their worn gloves. He appeared to be counting.

"I would say four days, maybe five. Before Christmas."

"That helps a lot. Anything unusual about his visit on that day?"

"Well, he brought the goodies, the same as always. But he was carrying a Santa suit. I gave him a hard time about that."

"Did he leave with the Santa suit?"

"Yes'm. He did. Laughed and joked a little, left the treats, then went on his way."

"Thank you, sir. Thank you very much. If you see Nick tell him, his friends and brother are looking for him. He disappeared just before Christmas."

The man's jaw dropped and Mava could see the plug of tobacco between his teeth and cheek. "You don't say! Yes'm, if I see him I sure will tell him."

Mava walked a half block to the east, where the bank was less steep before coming back to the sidewalk. At least one witness had seen Nick the evening on December twenty-third, and he had appeared to be fine.

Next, she walked west toward the bridge over the White River. The neighborhood to the south of Tenth Street was a shamble of clapboard cottages and small outbuildings. Some of them were probably outhouses, she realized. She saw women and children in some yards. One older girl hung semi-frozen laundry on a line. Mava decided to turn around, from Thomas's description of Nick's activities, this did not sound like the type of environment he had visited on his rounds.

That left the Fall Creek bridge, north of her apartment. A sharp wind attacked her neck. If she hadn't been in a hurry, she would've stopped at her place to pick up a scarf. Clouds were rolling in, suggesting that snow may fall in a couple of hours.

The Fall Creek bridge had lamps on both the north and south edges. St. Vincent Hospital stood on the north side of Fall Creek, which was as wide as a river. St. Vincent, where she'd spent her student days. That relatively carefree period of her life seemed ages ago. But the proximity to the place of her training brought her a sense of courage coupled with optimism.

She skirted the southwest lamppost and began her descent to the riverbank. There were three small shelters there. All were less well constructed than the shanties nearer the City Hospital. Mava heard nothing other than the sounds of traffic passing over the bridge. Then, a man in a tattered coat came out of the shelter nearest to the river. Mava could see newsprint peeking out of the coat's lapel. His breath took the form of fluffy frost. "Who are you?" he asked.

"I'm a friend of Nick's," Mava stood motionless as she spoke. "Do you know him? He sometimes brought doughnuts."

The man smiled at the word "doughnuts". "Yes, I know him. I saw him yesterday morning, though, and there weren't no doughnuts. He weren't wearing no coat, either. And he was acting crazy."

Mava felt her heart sink. She had to clear her throat before she could speak. "Why do you say he was acting crazy?"

"Huh." The man shrugged as if Mava should know the answer. "Well, like I said, lady, he weren't wearing a coat! And for another thing, he walked on the ice to cross the river. Must've been frozen solid enough. He could've drowned."

Mava shivered at his words. "Yes, he certainly could have. Thank you for the information. You've been helpful. In the meantime, if you see Nick, tell him to go home to his brother."

The man shook his head. "The last time I saw Nick, he didn't know who he was. I'm sure he forgot about any brother he had."

Mava couldn't think of anything more to say. She nodded and climbed up the river bank. Nick's situation sounded like combat stress. She'd nursed a few patients with that condition after battles in Europe. Some of them had been injured, others were physically unscathed, but mentally fragile. As a medic, Nick had probably seen some terrible things. Formerly healthy young soldiers…she found herself shaking her head. She didn't like to think of those images. Could a physical altercation on the street, the flash of a knife blade, or the sound of a gunshot have triggered something in Nick?

Mava climbed back to street level and crossed the bridge. Once on the opposite bank, she descended to the north edge of Fall Creek, and turned to face away from the river. She could see the upper story of St. Vincent's Hospital, with a cross at the peak of the roof over its main entrance. As the setting sun peeked out from behind a cloud, it shone directly on the white cross, making it reflect a silver-gold hue. Had Nick noticed the cross? Did he think of a church, a hospital or another place of refuge? Mava needed to find out. She trudged up the riverbank, across the street and through St. Vincent's main door.

A few people lingered in the lobby, putting on hats and gloves. A faint scent of disinfectant hung in the dry interior air. The pale green walls, the crucifix on the wall, the picture of St.Vincent next to the main entrance transported her back to student days, only four and half years ago. She'd changed so much since then.

She turned to her right, walked down a hallway, and entered a door marked "Men's Medical". A young nurse wearing a pointed white cap looked up at her. At first, her gaze was blank, but she blinked her eyes and the flash of recognition crossed her features. "Mava! I heard you'd enlisted. And now you're back."

Mava tried to manage a smile. "Hello, Veronica. Yes, I did enlist, and was stationed in Europe for a couple of years."

"So glad you're safe. Are you visiting someone on our ward?"

"Ron, don't think I'm crazy, but I'm hoping that I will recognize one of your patients. One of my coworkers is missing, a former soldier. He may be suffering from combat stress. He may not even know who he is."

Veronica's jaw dropped. "We have a patient that walked into the lobby yesterday, without a coat, wet shoes…no identification and unable to give us his name. He has a superficial gunshot wound to his right forearm."

"Is he a youngish man?" Mava's heart pounded.

"I would say so. He sleeps mostly. Sometimes he eats a little. Hasn't said much of anything."

"Can I see him?"

Veronica looked uncomfortable at the suggestion. "He's not supposed to have visitors. Doctor's orders."

"Please, Ron. His brother is sick with worry."

"Maybe you should bring his brother here."

"It would be difficult. His brother had polio, has a hard time walking." Mava tried to appear calm. *Come on, Ron. I need to see this man now! Don't get all pious on me.*

Veronica bit her lip. "All right. You can have a look at him. I just peeked in a minute ago, he was asleep." She pushed back her chair and stood.

Mava followed her to a bed at the farthest end of the ward, behind a screen. The corner of the ward was shadowy, and white sheets covered the patient up to his chin, but she could make out the features and the reddish-brown hair. No blood on the white sheets, no irregular shapes indicating splints or casts. Just a young man who appeared to be sleeping.

"Nick." She said his name aloud, without thinking.

Nick's eyelids fluttered, and he searched the room for the face belonging to the voice. His features wore a puzzled expression for a moment. Finally, he smiled. "Mava."

"You remember me." Mava struggled to keep her emotions in check.

Nick struggled to sit up. He looked at the bedclothes, the screen surrounding his bed. He lifted his right arm and looked at the bandage. His gaze came back to Mava.

"I know your name is Mava. But how do I know it?"

"We worked together at Ayres. You were Santa."

Nick's eyes widened. "How could I forget the prettiest girl at L. S. Ayres? Yes, the Santa Cottage…and the eighth floor." Nick looked at his surroundings, focusing on Veronica. "I'm not exactly sure how I got here. A hospital? Am I sick?" He paused.

Mava shook her head. "No, you've experienced something, but you're not sick. Not in the physical sense."

"I think Christmas must be over." Nick looked at Mava. She nodded.

"Are we into the new year yet?" He focused on Mava's eyes.

Veronica spoke up. "I'm encouraged! You have a sense of time. No, still several days to go until we ring in 1946."

"Good." Nick glanced at Veronica before stretching his arms overhead. "Because I've been making a plan for New Year's Eve." He winked at Mava.

She hoped the lighting was dim enough to hide her blush.

Self-Frosting Anise Cookies

These have been a favorite in my family at Christmas-time since my earliest childhood memories. The recipe has been passed down from my grandmother. These cookies are inexpensive to make and are relatively low in calories.

2 eggs (let warm to room temperature)

1 cup sugar

3/4 teaspoon anise extract

1 cup all-purpose flour

Grease cookie sheets.

Beat eggs on high speed in medium bowl for 4 minutes. (Don't skimp on any of the beating time.) Gradually add sugar, beating on high speed an additional 10 minutes, until thick. Add anise extract. Beat flour into mixture on low speed.

Drop dough by rounded teaspoonfuls onto prepared cookie sheets. Place in COLD oven and let set 8 to 12 hours or overnight.

Remove cookies from cold oven. Preheat oven to 350°F. Bake for 9 to 12 minutes (cookies will be dry but should not be brown). Use metal spatula and remove to wire rack and let cool completely, then store in covered tin.

Makes about three dozen

Into the Light Darkness Falls

By C. A. Paddock

One by one the members of our winter solstice circle walked to the fireplace and threw into the Yule log fire regrets, sorrows, sins, losses, angers, deaths, fears, illnesses, and failures from the past year—torn pieces of paper crumpled, stacked, folded, balled up—and watched as they were consumed by the flames. An absolution for the past year's shadows that darkened each member, a symbolic release of what was no longer wanted to make way for the new year and the return of the light.

When all were done, we recited in unison, "May the darkness of our soul's night be consumed by the year's coming light."

The solstice ceremony continued as we spoke aloud our creative and evergreen moments as well as the sacrifices we made during the past year. Near the end, Julie, my best friend and youngest member of the group, slipped out to prepare for the final part of the ceremony. We sang "Here Comes the Sun" (maybe not as well as the Beatles, but still in tune and in harmony) as she walked into the room dressed in a long white gown with a red sash belted around her waist. Perched on her head was a wreath made of small fir tree limbs placed with six lit plastic candles. Here was St. Lucia bringing light and sustenance to help us make it through the dark winter nights. Light from the candles reflected off the edges of the silver tray she carried which was piled with small s-shaped St. Lucia buns. She stopped to offer each person one of the saffron-infused raisin treats. Finally, she placed the tray with the remaining buns on a table decorated with red tapered candles and poinsettias. The celebration of the coming year's light came to an end.

The next morning I got up feeling renewed and ready for the rest of the holidays. As I was cleaning out the ashes from the fireplace and removing a chunk of the Yule log to save for next year's celebration, I reflected on how many years we had been gathering to celebrate the winter solstice.

It began ten years ago when Julie and I were talking about how we were both disillusioned with our respective churches. We wanted to be a part of something that not only acknowledged our Christian upbringings, but also affirmed our beliefs of the interdependence of all living things. So, Julie and I formed a group to explore this desire. Our group members came from different religious backgrounds, but we all sought one thing: to be able to celebrate our spirituality in our own way and to acknowledge the many universal truths that all religions share. To this end, we created rituals and gatherings to celebrate these truths. The winter solstice was one of our most popular ceremonies and for many, the start of their holiday seasons.

Even though I still celebrated Christmas and all its trappings, it's the winter solstice that made me feel closest to the mysteries of the universe. I loved it even more when it was held at my house. It's a chance to decorate with holly branches from my backyard, evergreens, mistletoe and lots of poinsettias.

Being preoccupied with my thoughts, I wasn't exactly paying attention to what I was doing until I noticed a few pieces of unburnt paper from the night before. As I pushed them back under the grate so they would burn next time, my eyes focused on the charred pieces. I realized with a growing sense of dread that the words "killed someone" and "River" had been untouched by the flames.

I stared at those words as my heart beat faster and my breath fell in line with its beat. Was I seeing those words correctly? I knew I was betraying a trust by just reading them. But murder was beyond that trust, wasn't it? I flashed on the ceremony the night before and what each member had said. I couldn't remember anything that would indicate a killer among us. Maybe this was a metaphor for overcoming a bad trait for purposes of the ritual. That was most likely the case. However, my mind kept going. What if I was wrong and whoever wrote it might get away with killing someone? But, it was hard to believe that someone in the group could succumb to such darkness.

I averted my eyes from the fireplace while I considered what to do. I couldn't go to the police. What would I say? Someone in my winter solstice ceremony group wrote that they killed somebody, but I didn't know who wrote it, who was killed or when it happened. And when the police heard the part about the fire ritual they would suspect we were some kind of devil worshipers and question the group as a whole.

Who could I even talk to about this? Anyone in our circle might have written this, except me. That left six others. But what if I confided in the very person who wrote it? I could give away the whole thing. But I couldn't just ignore it either. How could I meet with this group again knowing that one of them had written this and possibly committed one of the worst things imaginable?

On instinct I ran to the hall closet and grabbed a work glove and a plastic zip lock bag. I returned to the fireplace and gently removed the scrap of paper and dropped it into the baggie. I wasn't sure what I was going to do with it, but I wanted to keep it if I needed proof. Proof of what, I didn't know yet. I took the bag over to the oak roll-top desk in the corner of the dining room and placed it in a top drawer.

I walked into the kitchen with my mind still racing. I needed something to help me calm down. After breaking open a bottle of Oliver rosé wine, and nearly drinking the entire bottle, I decided that before I said anything to anyone, I needed to have a conversation with Bob. My husband wasn't part of the group and he was always the objective one when my worries and imagination ran amok. Maybe he could help advise me about what to do and tell me if I was crazy or what. But first I needed to outline the possibilities.

I grabbed a spiral notebook leftover from our kid's school days, found a clean sheet of paper and wrote down everyone who had been at the ceremony. When I finished, I reviewed the seven names: Anne (that's me), Julie, Sue, Morgan, Edith, Jackson, and Maya. Then I went back and started filling in what information I knew about everyone, except for me, of course.

I stared at the list and still couldn't fathom any one of them killing someone. And what about the word "River." What river? The White River? They were always finding bodies in the only waterway that ran through Indianapolis. But surely if someone in our group had anything to do with one of those bodies, the police would have been investigating. And wouldn't we have heard about it?

I needed to talk this out with Bob. I tipped the bottle of rosé and let the last drops slide over my tongue and down my throat. I plopped down on the loveseat my parents gave us when we got married and began to rub the loose blue threads on the arms while waiting for Bob to get home.

I must have fallen asleep because the next thing I felt was a tapping on my shoulder.

"Anne. Anne, wake up. You must have had a busy day."

"What? Huh?" I opened my eyes and looked up at Bob. He was smiling and holding the Oliver Winery bottle.

"I said you must have had a busy day, drinking the entire bottle by yourself!"

The words "killed someone" started to fly through my mind again and I sat up. "Bob, I'm so glad you're home! You won't believe what I found in our fireplace today!"

I proceeded to tell him about cleaning the fireplace and finding the charred paper. I went through the list I made so fast that he had to stop me several times. He even made me repeat the whole thing so he could "understand me right."

"I really need to talk this through with you," I told him, trying to slow down and catch my breath. "I don't know what to do. Should I call the police, or should I talk to everyone first? What if someone is dead and their family doesn't know? Or the body hasn't even been found yet? I can't believe that anyone I know would do such a thing."

"Whoa, there. We don't even know that someone was killed. Let's back up and start with the piece of paper. Can you show it to me?"

I went to the dining room, retrieved the plastic bag, and handed it to him. Bob stared at it for a few minutes as if he thought the entire phrase would come to him.

"At first, I was going to ask you if you recognized the handwriting. But I can see it's been typed. Is that unusual?"

"Not really. We want everyone to come prepared for the ceremony, that's why we send out a prep guide the week before. Most people bring their symbols to share, but a few may do it on the spot. Those people usually scribble out their regrets and disappointments on ripped pieces of paper just before their turn. Others have neatly folded stacks ready to go. Those strips could be typed just as easily as handwritten."

"What about the fire ceremony itself? I know the fire burning is symbolic, so could it be that someone just wrote those words to symbolize a loss or death of a part of his or her self—and maybe that realization came to them when they were sitting by a river."

"Possibly. But why would you call a part of you 'someone' and capitalize 'River' that way if that's what you meant. I would have written 'killed my ego down by the river,' or something like that."

"OK. So, there's a good chance that this isn't symbolic. And if someone did die, maybe it was an accident or something that happened a long time ago. Let's go through your list one more time and see if we can figure this out before you do anything." Bob glanced down at the list I had written. "First there's Julie…"

I interrupt Bob before he could say anything else. "I don't think Julie could have done it. Julie's one of our closest friends. I've known her since high school and then we became good friends when we went to Butler. She would've told me if she accidently killed someone."

"Maybe something happened at one of her parties that she managed through her event company."

"'Parties Done Right' doesn't mean 'Parties to Kill Someone by the River.' Even if something awful had happened at one of her parties, I'm sure she would have told me about it and gone straight to the police."

"Alright but remember someone here last night had to have written it. And we know it wasn't you. I think we need to keep her on the list until we figure out what this means." Bob picked up the list and read the next name.

Sue—registered nurse, works for Life's Journey Hospice Care. Originally from Michigan but has lived in Indiana for twenty years. Married with three grown children.

"Sue. I know Sue, too," Bob said, "from all she did for your dad six years ago. I can't imagine someone who is so kind and compassionate, killing another human being. Though, I suppose in her job she sees lots of suffering and the whole point of hospice care is to ease a person's suffering and let them die with dignity. I know I have heard of nurses who 'help' their patients along, but that just doesn't seem like Sue." Bob raised his hands and made air quotations with his fingers when he said help.

"I agree with you. Sue came every day at the end and always talked directly to Dad even when he was out of it. Her voice was so soothing and caring. I don't know what we would've done without her." My eyes started to tear up as I thought of the last days with my dad. "Besides if she did something like that, it would be in a hospital bed, not a river, don't you think? And she's been with our group since that first winter solstice after Dad died."

"Right. Let's move on. What do you know about Morgan?"

"I don't know much about him. Julie knows him better. He's a psychologist who specializes in dream therapy. Julie met him in a group she used to be in where everyone analyzed their dreams. She's been his client for a couple of years now. His office is in the front part of his bungalow in Broad Ripple. His partner, Jeffrey, lives with him, I believe. Here again, I can't imagine someone whose job it is to help others would kill someone. But I will have to ask Julie about him."

"Maybe this is about one of Morgan's dreams," Bob reasoned. "No need to bring in the police for something that was only a dream."

"I guess that is feasible, since this is the first time he's participated."

Bob looked at the ruled paper again.

Edith—professional violinist with the Indianapolis Symphony Orchestra. Friend from First Unitarian Church. Founding circle member.

"Next is Edith. She was the first person we met when we started going to church. She's a vital part of the church and community. But she can be rather outspoken in certain situations. Remember the time she got up in front of the congregation during the announcements and declared that if people didn't start signing up to help with Coffee Hour, she would sell all the cups and urns and give the money to the Martin Luther King Street Food Pantry?" He chuckled.

"I remember that. She's stubborn when she doesn't get her way or when she thinks an injustice is being done. But she sure can make that violin sing. I love it when she plays during the Sunday service," I paused, scrunching my forehead as I thought. "Edith was a founding member of the winter solstice circle, but we don't really know much about her background, do we? And she does have a temper. Maybe there is more to her than we know."

Bob cocked his head. "You're right. We don't know much about her background. Although did I hear that she was married once, but her husband disappeared on the day of their first wedding anniversary?"

"I think that was just a rumor. One time when Edith was here helping to decorate for the winter solstice ceremony, she alluded to the fact that her husband had run off with her best friend. But she didn't say anymore, and Julie and I didn't ask."

"Well, it sounds suspicious to me. I'm putting an asterisk by her name. Let's keep going. What about Jackson? I've only met him a couple of times at church. But he seems like a nice enough guy."

"Jackson is a friend of Edith's. I think they met at the symphony. And that's why he's been at church a few times, when Edith has invited him. Jackson was a criminal defense attorney in Carmel until he couldn't live with himself anymore defending people he knew were guilty. He believed everyone had a right to an attorney, but it couldn't be him anymore. His wife was having an affair while he worked long hours and he just couldn't take it anymore. He left her and his job and went to Sedona, Arizona, to stay at a spiritual retreat for a while to try to find his way. He seems to have come back a different person, as Edith tells it. He's been coming to the winter solstice ceremony for about four years."

"Maybe someone from his past killed someone else by a river," said Bob. "That would make sense. It could have been one of his clients who did it but got off. Jackson knew he was guilty but couldn't do anything because he was defending him. Jackson hasn't been able to tell anyone all these years because of attorney-client privilege and wanted the weight of knowing the truth lifted from him. He used the fire ceremony to rid him of his guilt."

"I like that. It sure makes more sense than Edith killing off her husband, or Sue helping along a patient's death, or even Morgan murdering someone. Maybe I can call Edith and see what she knows about Jackson's cases and see if any of them involved a murder by a river. It's worth a shot." It would sure ease my mind, I thought, if I found out that Jackson was alleviating his guilt over something one of his clients did.

"I guess we better talk about the last person on your list if we want to do this right. Maya. I know you've been good friends since that writing workshop. Do you think she could have written it?" Bob asked.

"No, I don't. She's been coming to the ceremony for five years. She works for the Indiana Writers Center now and is such an amazing poet and artistic, ethereal person. I just love how she can turn ordinary words into detailed photos in the mind. Or how she can put enough twist on an old saying to give it new meaning. Her creativity helps generate my imagination and helps me find the right words when I write. Her friendship has been a blessing to me. I just don't know how she could have done anything so vile."

"Perhaps Maya wrote a poem and she hated it. She saw it as one of her failures and wanted to burn it. All this drama for nothing."

"Hmm. Possible I suppose. But my bet is on Jackson. That does make the most sense to me. Thanks for taking time to talk through these with me. My mind was going a thousand places before you got home. I knew you would help me sort this all out. I'll try to call Edith tomorrow about Jackson."

That night I tossed and turned unable to sleep. By the time I got up the next morning, my head hurt and my muscles throbbed. I knew the bottle of wine had caused the headache, but it was my dreams that kept me turning all night.

Instead of focusing on my sleepless night, I recounted the discussion Bob and I had yesterday. He was right. It was probably Jackson who had written those words. I needed to call Edith for any information she might have on him. However, the foggy feeling from my dreams still clung to me like an old worn cardigan. I decided first to contact my best friend to see if she could help me shrug off this sensation.

I texted Julie to see if she could come over. She replied immediately and said she would be over in the next half hour. She always made me feel better with her warm, compassionate personality, and I could confide in her what I discovered since I had convinced myself that Jackson had done it.

When she arrived, she gave me a big hug and told me how much the ceremony the other night meant to her. "Every year I just dread the holidays, but once we celebrate the winter solstice I feel in the spirit of things and look forward to the new year."

"I agree. But this year has turned out a little different for me. That's why I wanted you to come over. I didn't sleep well last night because of horrible dreams. I know why I had the dreams, but I need to confide in you about what caused them."

We sat down on the couch as I proceeded to tell her about finding the unburnt strip of paper and what was written on it. I told her about Bob and me talking about each person who attended the ceremony and reassured her that we knew she couldn't have done it. I noticed while I was talking to her that she had grown very still and hadn't said a word since I began. Her eyes were focused on her black pants. She glanced up when I stopped talking. I could see tears had formed in the corners of her eyes.

"I need to tell you something, Anne. I've kept this a secret for too many years. Through my therapy sessions with Morgan, I realized it was time to let this go," Julie whispered, water dripping from her cheeks. "Do you remember Jody Brown from high school?"

"Sure. She was the head of the cheerleading squad who killed herself just before the start of our senior year. I didn't know her very well though."

"I don't know if you knew this or not, since we didn't hang around with each other in high school, but Wade dated her after he broke up with me. I didn't like her, of course. I was jealous of her and blamed her for Wade dumping me."

"I remember Wade. He was in my Algebra class. I never could understand what you saw in him. He was so arrogant."

Julie got up and started to pace. "I realize that now… but then, I had our life all planned out—Wade's and mine. Marriage after graduating from IU, then get the hell out of Indiana. But Jody had to hook her claws into him in Chemistry class. She always was asking him for help. And by the end of the school year, Wade came to me and said he wanted to take a break during the summer before we went to college. Right after graduation I saw him at The Dairy sitting on the stone bench sharing an ice cream cone with Jody. Then it seemed that everywhere I went, they were there. I couldn't escape them. Her parents divorced that summer and she leaned on Wade even more."

"Oh, yes, The Dairy. My first job and the only place in town to meet your friends on a warm Saturday night," I interjected. I smiled up at her but stopped when I saw her lips quiver.

"The night she died, I saw them together again at The Dairy. This time, though, she was hitting Wade's chest with her fists and yelling at him. I couldn't tell what she was saying, and I didn't care. I just drove on by and went to a friend's house. The friend offered me some speed and I washed the pills down with cherry vodka and Mountain Dew. When I left, I was flying high, and ready to take on anyone who got in my way."

She paused and looked me in the eyes. "I haven't done any drugs since that night. And of course, I would never get in a car and drive like that now, but back then you know that's what we all did." She began to pace again.

"I heard there was a party at Old Jedidiah's farm and decided to head there. When I came to the rickety metal bridge on County Line Road over the Big Blue River, I saw Jody sitting on the edge. I stopped and rolled down my window and yelled at her, 'Whatcha doin' out here, Bitch?'"

"She just flipped me the finger. Well that made me mad. So, I put the car into park and got out, my skin was crawling and tingling, and I was itching to fight. I said to her, 'What was that you did? Don't you ever do that to me again if you know what's good for you!' She yelled back. 'Wade broke up with me tonight. Are you happy now? Just leave me be.' And just like that I pushed her off the bridge. I heard her scream as I slid around the front of my car and into the driver's seat. I sped off and never looked back." Julie stopped making a path in the carpet and looked at my wide-open mouth.

"The next day when I heard that her body was found in the river, I knew it was because of me. But I didn't tell anyone I was out there that night. Everybody said that she had become despondent after her folks divorced and her father moved away. Then Wade broke up with her. When they found her diary stating she wanted to die, I figured she was on the bridge to jump anyway. And when her death was ruled a suicide, I just kept quiet." Julie sat back down on the couch next to me.

"After that I decided to go to Butler instead of IU. Remember, Anne, I was a lot different in high school than I am now. I put on my happy-go-lucky face, but deep down inside this has been eating away at me for years. So much so I had planned to go to Morristown and tell her mom what happened, but then I heard that she had died."

"And her dad passed away when we were in college," I whispered, looking down at the floor.

"I feel awful about what I did in high school, but what can I do about it now except to release the burden of knowing what I did?"

Julie waited for me to speak. The tick, tick of seconds going by punctuated the time. I tried to think of what to say.

"I'm at a loss for words," was all I uttered. I wanted to scream "How could have you done something so horrible and not tell anyone?" but I couldn't say a word. I didn't know what I would have done in her shoes.

We sat on the loveseat as the sound of the second hand filled the silence. Finally, Julie stood. I gazed up at her, black lines streaked her face. "You need to tell the police in Morristown. I can go with you. Or if you want me to go tell them I can. But we have to do something."

"No, I can't. And you won't either. I thought you were my best friend and you'd understand. But I can see by your reaction you think I'm wrong. I'll go now." And with that she turned and went out the door.

My mind reeled. Wasn't I right that she had to tell the police? Or if not her, should I? But what purpose would it serve now? Everyone in Jody's family was gone, and I didn't even know if anyone involved with the case was still around. My thoughts kept whirling. I couldn't believe she'd never told me about this. I knew we didn't run in the same circles in high school, but when we became close in college, I thought we told each other everything. She always seemed to have it all together and the perfect life. How could I not have known? She must have buried that deep inside her all these years. What should I do? What would happen to her, if the police found out? Would she go to jail after all this time? Surely, she has suffered enough keeping that secret.

With my head throbbing even more, I went to look for another bottle of wine. And with a little help from Oliver again, I knew what I had to do.

That evening I told Bob I was sorry I made such a big deal of the whole thing and reminded him that the point of the fire burning ceremony was to privately purge anything heavy in our hearts. After all these years we never discussed what we burned outside of our group and I was foolish to break that sacred bond now. He nodded in agreement with a look of relief in his eyes, kissed me, and said, "Now it's time for bed."

"I think I'll stay up for a little bit while the fire burns out. You go on and I'll join you soon."

I watched the embers glow for a minute, then got up, walked to the dining room desk, opened the drawer, and took out the plastic bag. Back at the fireplace, I pulled apart the zipped bag and removed the piece of charred paper. I slid back the metal screen and threw the paper onto the hot ashes. As I watched a little flame erupt, flare bright and die, I whispered, "May the light consume the darkness held within these words and release us from their burden."

I shut the fireplace doors and headed to the stairs.

St. Lucia Buns

(Recipe by King Arthur Flour)

1 cup milk

1/4 teaspoon saffron threads, lightly crushed

1/2 cup butter

4 1/2 cups King Arthur unbleached all-purpose flour

1 tablespoon instant yeast

1/4 cup potato flour or 1/2 cup instant potato flakes

1 1/2 teaspoons salt

1/3 cup granulated sugar

3 large eggs

1 teaspoon vanilla extract

Topping

1 large egg white (reserved from dough) mixed with 1 tablespoon cold water

Coarse pearl sugar, optional

Golden raisins, optional

In a small saucepan set over medium heat, heat the milk and saffron to a simmer; remove from the heat and stir in the butter. Set the mixture aside to allow the butter to melt and cool to lukewarm, 30 to 35 minutes. You can reduce the milk's cooling time by about 10 minutes by refrigerating it.

In a large bowl or the bowl of a stand mixer, whisk together the yeast, flours, salt and sugar. Pour the lukewarm milk and butter mixture over the dry ingredients.

Separate one of the eggs and set the white aside to use later. Add the 2 whole eggs, 1 egg yolk, and the vanilla. Mix to combine, then knead for about 7 minutes by mixer, or 10 minutes by hand, until the dough is smooth and supple.

Place the dough in a lightly greased bowl, cover it, and let it rise for 1 hour, or until it's quite puffy, though not necessarily doubled in bulk.

Gently deflate the dough and divide it into 12 equal pieces. Shape the pieces of dough into rough logs, and let them rest, covered, for about 10 minutes. This gives the gluten a chance to relax.

Roll each log into a 15" to 18" rope. They'll shrink once you stop rolling; that's OK. Shape each rope into an "S" shape. Tuck a golden raisin into the center of each of the two side-by-side coils, if desired.

Place the buns on a lightly greased or parchment-lined baking sheet, leaving an inch or so between them. Cover them, and let them rise for about 30 minutes, until they're noticeably puffy, but definitely not doubled. While they're rising, preheat the oven to 375°F.

Brush each bun with some of the egg white/water glaze. Sprinkle with coarse white Swedish pearl sugar, if desired.

Bake the buns until they're golden brown, about 18 to 20 minutes. If you've used raisins, tent them with foil for the final 3 minutes, to prevent the raisins from burning.

Remove the buns from the oven and transfer them to a rack to cool.

Makes 12 large buns

Killing Santa Claus

By MB Dabney

rake grunted and heaved with each step as he hauled the two large plastic containers up from the basement. And with each step, he silently cursed his wife.

It was true Shelly was the love of Drake's life, her beauty and mere presence made his life infinitely more enjoyable. But when they moved into the house back in the spring, it was Shelly who instructed the movers to stack the Christmas decoration containers in a corner of the basement, instead of an enclosed, first-floor storage area. And with just one small child and Shelly often busy at work, Drake knew all along he'd probably be the one hauling Christmas gear up from the basement.

The foreknowledge didn't keep him from grumbling about it.

"Here I am, getting this crap out every year...by myself," he voiced to no one as he opened the basement door into the kitchen. But to his surprise, there was someone there.

"Thank you, baby, for finally bringing those things up," Shelly cheerfully said as she sauntered over to deliver a small kiss to his full lips, and then a kiss to his clean-shaven head. "My big strong police detective, haulin' up all those big, heavy containers."

He let the playful comment slide.

"What are you doing home so early?"

Shelly reached into a bag of groceries on the counter, then opened the fridge to start putting things away. "I had a surgery cancel at the last minute, so I decided to head to the grocery and come home early."

Drake couldn't help but smile at Shelly as they put away groceries, one of the most mundane of everyday tasks. Even in blue hospital scrubs, she was still a looker, just as much as when they married two decades earlier.

They moved into a modest, four-bedroom house shortly after her promotion to assistant head of pediatrics because it was near her job at All-Children's Hospital of Indianapolis. On her salary, they could afford pricier digs. But a fancier house would appear unseemly for a police detective, despite Shelly's earnings.

The neighbors, however, were thrilled to have a large black police officer on the block. At six-two and 250 solid, as he put it, Drake was a reassuring or menacing presence, depending on which side of the law you were on.

They were both startled when a neighbor suddenly appeared, banging frantically on the patio door.

"Help me, please," she said, pointing behind her back toward the street. "It's my husband Henry. Help me, please."

Despite the cold outside, Drake and Shelly left the house without coats and ran behind the woman, who kept babbling on about her husband.

"Just got home. The car. The garage. Engine on."

Three doors down, they rushed up a driveway. The garage door was up and inside the garage was a car with the motor running. A man was slumped inside.

Drake opened the car door and Shelly reached inside to check the man's pulse. She turned back and shook her head, confirming what was obvious to Drake.

Henry Gibson was dead.

His widow's wails reverberated throughout the couple's garage.

᙮ᘿ ᙮ᘿ ᙮ᘿ

"Did you know the guy, Drake?" his partner asked the next morning over coffee at their adjoining desks, one with a nameplate that said Drake Curtis and the other Morgan Barrie.

"No. Not really," Drake said, taking a sip of his coffee, then stirring in more sugar from a packet. "I'd say 'hi' and give him a wave when I saw him or his wife but I barely knew either of them. I mostly only remember their names because they are the block captains."

"Carbon monoxide. Wow. But there are worse ways to commit suicide." Barrie, like Drake, worked homicides.

"Yeah, but I can't wrap my head around this one," Drake said.

Barrie shuffled papers around on her desk. "You think too much. Some things are as they appear. The guy was depressed and killed himself. Happens all the time."

"Could be, but there was no note, according to the officers on the scene." Drake scratched his bald head. "And he was generally cheerful when I saw him. Didn't seemed depressed."

"You'd think, but until a month ago he was out of work. Got laid off from a management job back in January. Only found a part-time gig lately. That affects people," Lt. W. Brockman Boyce, who just walked up, said. He took the seat in the chair next to Drake's desk.

"How do you know that? This guy isn't some sort of criminal. No need for any profiling, though it's your job," Drake said.

"Ahhhh," Boyce started. He didn't speak for several beats. "It was in the police report. I only read it because I heard folks saying you were on the scene of a suicide near your house."

Because their captain walked hard on her heels, the trio heard her coming seconds before she arrived. She was a very no-nonsense commander and got straight to the point. No unnecessary greetings.

"They found a body out in Irvington. Ellenberger Park. I want you two on it. Dispatch will give you the exact location," she said. "And Detective Curtis, you take point."

They acknowledged the captain and rose to leave. But she looked at Lt. Boyce. "Don't you have some cases to profile? Work's not gonna get done on its own."

As was usual when they rode together, Drake drove. He didn't turn on the lights. There was no need to rush. The victim was already dead.

"You get the Christmas gear put up on your house last night?" Barrie asked.

"Didn't have time. It was too dark by the time I got back home from across the street."

"You'd better get it done soon. Snow last Saturday was an aberration for this early in December. But bad weather could come at any time."

Drake drove past a car without a visible license plate. Any other time, he would have pulled them over.

"Tonight or tomorrow I'll get up on the roof with the Santa, sleigh, and reindeer and set them up. I hate that part, fighting those damned decorations."

"You finish Christmas shopping?"

"Not yet. Shelly's assigned me to find some fancy doll for Dana. But they're sold out everywhere. I can't find it. Tried online and everything," Drake said as he turned off New York and onto Emerson. "I'll try to hit a couple of stores this afternoon if I can sneak out a little early. To Shelly, the doll's the more important thing."

"I'll bet," Barrie said. "What's with this doll?"

"I don't know. Shelly says it's a Holiday Elegance Barbie. The dark skin one, of course. Long black hair and dressed in a red velvet coat with white fur trim. Like what a Santa wears."

Drake parked a short distance from the park entrance on St. Clair.

There wasn't a cloud in the sky and the bright sun warmed the air. Drake unbuttoned his coat as he and his partner made their way over uneven ground to a wooded area where there was a lot of police activity. Patches of snow scattered about were reminders of the previous weekend's storm.

Ducking yellow police tape, the pair approached a uniformed officer. "Detectives," was all the officer said as he walked them down a slight incline to a crop of spruce trees. Resting under a particularly large tree was a man decked out in full Santa Claus regalia— black boots, bright red pants, and a red coat trimmed in white fur and closed with a black, buckled belt. His fake beard was as white as a nearby pile of snow.

Drake stared down silently at the man, whose legs were positioned in an unnaturally awkward way. There were two nice little bullet holes in his chest, over where his heart would be.

"My, my, my, what have we got here, Sergeant?" Barrie asked.

Pointing to a couple of officers talking to a tall, middle-aged female holding a frisky dog on a leash, he said, "A woman walking her dog this morning on the path over there saw the body and contacted the police. We're still interviewing her."

Drake stooped down to the body but was careful not to touch anything. He looked back up to the sergeant. "How long ago was he found?"

"'Bout sixty minutes."

"Anybody touch anything?" Barrie asked.

"I searched him for ID but other than that, no," the sergeant said.

Drake rose again to stand next to his partner, who had a little notebook out. "Who is he?" Drake asked.

The officer ticked off the information without assistance. "According to his driver's license, he's Raphael Hernandez, fifty-seven. Hispanic male. Five-foot-nine, 200 pounds. Lives on Robey Drive in Clermont."

"Arrest record?" Barrie asked.

"Initially, none I have found. I figure you guys'll dig deeper."

"What was he doing here? Any drug activity in this area?" Drake asked.

"Not here. It's a quiet neighborhood, with families and kids. The drug problem is back towards town. Around 10th street."

"Doesn't look like a robbery," Barrie said.

"Nothing was taken as far as we can see. He's still wearing a watch, wedding ring, and his wallet was on him. Back pocket."

"How'd he get here? You find a car?" Drake asked.

Barrie pointed to the ground, which indicated tire tracks from near the victim all the way back to the street.

"Looks like he was dumped here," Barrie said. Drake and the officer nodded.

"We haven't found a car. Only the tire tracks over there," the officer said, again pointing to the edge of the road.

"How long's he been dead?" Drake asked.

The answer came from behind him.

"Based on lividity, I'd say twelve hours, more or less," said an older man in civilian clothes wearing white plastic gloves and pulling a stretcher.

Drake smiled. "Good to see you, Mac. What do you think happened here?"

"Clearly, the man was shot," the coroner said in a cheeky voice. "But can't say more than that until I have him on my autopsy table. Mind if I take the body now, detective?"

The police sergeant and Barrie looked directly at Drake.

"No, go 'head. I think we're pretty much done here," Drake said. To Barrie, he said, "Catch a ride back downtown. See if he's in the system and check out his bank statements. I'm going out to Clermont and see what I can find."

"Detective Curtis, a word please," Mac said to Drake as he turned to leave.

The detective and the coroner walked a short distance from the others. Much older than Drake, the coroner displayed a paternal attitude toward the detective.

"You were right this morning. It wasn't a suicide last night," Mac said in a low voice. "Haven't had time for a full autopsy but I looked over the body and observed a small pin prick hole in his neck. Barely visible. I think someone injected your neighbor with a strong sedative. He might have succumbed to carbon monoxide asphyxiation in the car but the sedative would have kept him from moving and seeking help. He was murdered."

❧ ❧ ❧

Drake drove to Clermont to interview the most recent victim's widow and was grateful the man's two youngest children, both high school students, weren't home yet.

"Raphie had no enemies," Maria Hernandez said, her shoulders rising and falling as she wept. She wiped her nose with a tissue. "He was a good man. Everyone loved him."

The house was warm and comfortable and there were photos of the couple's five children scattered about on every flat surface.

Drake got a clear understanding of the man—husband, father, non-smoker, infrequent drinker. A good provider until he was laid-off last summer as a machinist mate at a welding shop in Speedway.

"And what is this?" Drake asked as he picked a photo which was different from the rest. It showed perhaps two dozen men, all in varying stages of roundness. White beards hid the lower portion of most of their faces.

Marie Hernandez walked over, looked at the picture and struggled keeping in control. "It was at Santa Claus School in Kris Kringle, Indiana. Back in October. Raphie went and that's the graduation picture. He's on the second row."

She lost the battle and started crying again as she replaced the picture on the mantle.

"Raphie was a proud man and he loved being Santa Claus. For the kids. The school helped him get a steady job at the mall in Greenwood this Christmas."

"It's a long drive from here to work. Any idea why he was in Ellenberger Park last night? It's not near home or work."

She shook her head no.

After a few more questions, Drake thanked her and left.

With a few minutes on his hands, Drake stopped at two toy stores in the trip back to the office but didn't find what he needed.

Damn. Gotta find that doll. Cuttin' out early to put up SC, Drake texted Shelly.

Good. B careful, she replied.

At his desk, Drake verified Hernandez's employment—according to the mall manager, he was a model employee—and that Hernandez left alone last night when the mall closed. No criminal record, small banking account, modest credit rating that took a hit in the last six months as he struggled to pay all his bills.

Because no car was discovered at the scene, they issued an all-points bulletin for Hernandez's car—a blue, late-model Ford.

Drake had just informed his captain he was heading out early when Boyce wandered over to his desk. Drake was collecting his paperwork and tried his best to ignore the smart-dressing lieutenant.

"Caught another dead one, I hear," Boyce said, tapping the side of his leg in a nervous gesture. "Santa Claus."

"Yes, well, that's what we do down here in homicide."

"I wonder who'd want to kill Father Christmas," Boyce chortled without displaying any real interest in the question.

Drake stood and picked up his coat. "I guess we'll have to find out."

∾ ∾ ∾

Back home, an unseasonably warm December sun welcomed Drake outside as he used a rope to haul a large plastic Santa up to the roof, temporarily anchoring it to the chimney. Then he went back down the ladder and tied a rope around the remaining decorations.

Back on the roof, he was maneuvering the four-foot Santa when a heavy wind gust caught it, sending the Santa tumbling down the roof where it hit the ladder. The impact tipped the ladder, which seemed to hang in the air for the briefest of moments before falling to the ground. When it hit, the ladder smashed the Santa Claus.

"Damn. My second dead Santa of the day," he muttered to himself.

Drake reached for the cellphone he normally carried on his belt. It wasn't there. He had left it in its charging stand in the kitchen. He was at home alone and stranded on the roof—without a phone.

"Damnit," he said, this time aloud.

"Howdy, neighbor." A man with a cheerful disposition and a short, neatly trimmed grayish-white beard called up to him from the yard. He was slightly shorter than Drake—perhaps six-foot— and very soft through the middle. He was pinchable, the type of person people liked to hug.

"I saw you up there from next door," he said, surveying the ladder and the destroyed decoration. "Looks like you could use some help."

"Well, I guess I do. I'm the only one home and I left my cell phone in the house."

The guy picked up the ladder, positioned it against the house and climbed up. "Unfortunate. But I'm always happy to be of service," he said as he reached the roof. "Let's see what we got."

"Thank you, uh..." Drake started, wishing silently he remembered the correct name. "Jim, isn't it?"

"Joel. Joel Kerstman's the name," he said with a cheerfulness that spoke of a lifetime of amusement.

They made quick work of stringing the lights and attaching the reindeer and Santa sleigh, minus the Claus, to the roof, talking as they went along.

"I'll take those," Kerstman said, indicating the wire and clamps used to anchor the decorations. "You're a policeman, right?"

"A detective. Homicide," Drake said, handing over the items before going back to his work.

"Sounds so exciting. And you're off today?"

"No. I left early. Needed to finish this before dark and before it gets too cold again," Drake said, then added, "Hand me the hammer, please."

Kerstman stopped. He stroked his beard briefly, staring at Drake. "You don't seem to be enjoying this."

Drake looked at his neighbor. He hoped he could convey an understanding of the situation. "Look, I have a stressful job and a lot is going on right now. So, I probably appear somewhat distracted. I do this for my daughter and my wife. But especially for Dana. I just don't know how much longer she's going to believe in all this. In Santa Claus. In all the wonder."

"Why not?"

"I stopped believing around her age when I didn't get the carpentry set I badly wanted. I wrote Santa and even visited him at a department store. I said all I wanted was that carpentry set," Drake said. "And then I didn't get it."

The watch on Joel's arm beeped and he checked it. Then he started for the ladder. "I've got homemade chocolate chip cookies in the oven. Time for them to come out. You're mostly done up here."

"Go ahead. And thanks for the help," Drake said.

Once Kerstman was on the ladder and about to go down, he

looked back at Drake. "I hope your daughter gets her toy. It's sad when a child loses that Christmas wonder."

❦ ❦ ❦

Drake had everything put away by the time his wife and seven-year-old daughter got home. Dana was thrilled with the outdoor decorations on the house.

"I love the lights, Daddy. What happened to Santa? I thought you were gonna put up Santa," Dana said, nearly in a single breath.

"I had a little trouble with Santa but everything else looks good, right?" he asked, while giving his wife a glance that said, 'Don't ask.'

"My friend Stacey said I'm a big baby for still believing in Santa Claus. She said Santa's not gonna bring me my doll," she whimpered.

"He's going to bring your doll, baby, I promise," Shelly said, giving a questioning stare to Drake, who backed away without saying a word. "Don't you worry, baby. You've been good this year and Santa knows it."

As a career law enforcement officer, Drake had faced many dangers on the job. Some scared him and some did not. But the look on Shelly's face was dangerous and scary. It said, "You'll do this or there will be hell to pay."

Drake had trouble sleeping that night.

❦ ❦ ❦

By the week before Christmas, Drake was no closer to finding who killed Hernandez than he was to finding Dana's doll. When he arrived at his office on the morning just three days before Christmas, he sat at his desk, reached into a drawer, retrieved a bottle of antacid and took a swig. It was a new ritual.

"Heartburn?" Barrie asked.

"Like you wouldn't believe," Drake said.

"Maybe it's not just work. You should go see a doctor. You know, this is the time of year for heart attacks," Barrie said.

Drake ignored her. On his computer was the previous night's police reports and two items had Drake's attention. A non-fatal shooting and a deadly hit-and-run.

"It says here a man dressed as Santa was ringing a bell and collecting donations for the Salvation Army outside a grocery store on the eastside when shots rang out," Drake said.

Barrie picked up a cup of coffee, took a sip, then said, "Yeah, I read that just before you got in. Dark-colored car drove up, someone inside, thought to be a man…our victim wasn't sure…fired several rounds. Car drove off. All the shots missed. But they recovered a couple of the bullets and ballistics is running tests."

"And the car?" Drake asked.

"The victim ducked and couldn't give a description. No one else got a good look," Barrie said. "What are you thinking?"

"More than two hours later, a dark-colored car, thought to be a Ford, runs a guy over across from the Castleton Mall on 82nd street. Kills him." Drake leaned back in his chair and closed his eyes. "Something doesn't seem right."

Boyce walked up, looking as dapper as ever. "Murder or attempted murder is always a bit odd, I think. But it's what keeps us in business. If you ask me, it's the season. Psychos come out at Christmastime. It's all that holiday stress. They have to relieve it."

Boyce briefly paused as if in wonder. "I enjoy a psychopath's mind."

"What happened to you growing up?" Barrie said dismissively.

"Is that the sort of in-depth professional judgment we are paying you for?" the captain asked Boyce as she strolled in.

Before Boyce could answer, Drake sat up and asked, "Who'd

you assign this to?"

"The hit-and-run?"

"Yeah."

"Peterson. He's out interviewing people now. You got something?"

Drake grabbed his phone and called Detective Peterson's cell. "A hunch," he said as he waited for the call to connect.

The conversation was short and the others waited as Drake confirmed mostly what was already in the report. The victim was black, mid-40s, lived on the northside. Married, no kids. He was alone at the time heading for a bus stop. It was shortly after 10 p.m.

"Where did he work," Drake said and waited for an answer. "Bingo! Thanks." He hung up the phone.

"Where?" Barrie asked.

"The mall. Castleton had just closed for the night. The victim, Charles Livingston, was the mall Santa," Drake said. "Now we have two dead Santas and the attempted murder of a third. Can't be a coincidence."

Drake got up. "I'm going down to the evidence locker to look through Livingston's belongings."

"I'll go with you," Boyce said. "Might be something there to help me profile who's doing this."

"Get going," the captain said to Drake and Boyce. She turned to Barrie, "Detective, I want you to look up everything there is to know about all three of these guys. Cross-check for any connections. Education, employment, military service. Dig until you find something."

The evidence locker was in the basement of the building in a caged area. Drake retrieved a box with Livingston's things and signed for it. He took it over to a nearby counter, opened it and took out the contents.

Nothing surprising. Wallet, wedding ring, watch, cell phone.

Hand sanitizer. Breath mints. Drake flipped through the wallet. ID, credit cards, a library card, a transit pass, $57 in cash, family pictures. And...

"What's that?" Boyce asked.

"Evidence," Drake said with a smile as he held up a miniature copy of the photograph he saw in the Hernandez house. The picture of the men who graduated from Santa Claus school. He studied the picture closely. "Oh my god. I can't believe it."

"What is it?" Boyce said.

"Another connection," Drake said, handing the photo to Boyce as he headed for the door. "Put the stuff in the box and sign it back in. Thanks."

"Where are you going?"

"I got another hunch."

⌁⌁ ⌁⌁ ⌁⌁

"Hey," Drake said to Barrie as he reached his desk. "You find anything yet?"

"No," she said.

"Well, I found something." He picked up the phone and dialed.

"Hello, Mrs. Gibson. This is Drake Curtis from across the street."

"Oh yes. Of course," she said. An embarrassed hesitation followed. "Uh, I'm so sorry, uh, I haven't thanked you and your wife for all your help and kindness when Henry, uh, passed away. It's just I've been busy. But the bouquet of flowers were beautiful. And the Christmas Toffee Bars your wife brought over were so thoughtful."

Drake didn't want to sound rude but he was in the hurry. "You're quite welcome but that's not why I called."

"Oh?" she said.

"I have a couple of questions," Drake said. "Your husband lost his job earlier this year, right? But I think you said he was working again."

"Yes, he worked part-time visiting patients at a couple of hospitals several days a week," she said.

"What was his job? What did he do?"

"He dressed up as..." she started.

"Santa Claus," they said together.

"How'd you know?"

"I have one more question," Drake said. "Did he attend a Santa Claus school?"

"A couple of months ago, yes," she replied.

"Thank you very much, Mrs. Gibson. You have our sympathies, of course. And if you ever need anything, please just stop over."

Drake hung up but to Barrie, he said, "Now there are four victims. Three dead and one shot at. There could be more. You check the surrounding counties for every homicide in the last three months. See if there are any other Santas. And check again for Hernandez's car. I bet it's involved, too."

Drake swiveled around in the chair and faced his computer. A few clicks on his keyboard and up popped the website for The Santa Claus School. He scrolled through the site, checking its home page, the links to his history, mission, staff and finally its board. And it was there he discovered a familiar face.

Joel Kerstman.

Drake was shocked but recovered quickly. "Barrie, get your coat. Let's go."

Detective Morgan Barrie was out of her chair in an instant. "Where we going?"

"To my neighbor's house. To confront the killer."

While he wasn't expecting it, Drake also wasn't surprised to see a blue, late-model Ford in Kerstman's driveway.

"I bet it belongs to Raphael Hernandez and has front-end damage," Drake said.

He signaled for two uniformed officers to head around back while he and Barrie approached the front door, which was ajar. They both pulled out their guns. Drake raised his hand and silently counted down from three with his fingers. Then they both entered the house.

They moved in slowly, searching as they went. Finally, in the kitchen, they found Kerstman in a chair, his hands tied behind his back. He appeared amazingly calm, almost jovial, despite the dire situation he faced. Standing next to the kitchen table, wearing rubber gloves and preparing an injection with a hypodermic needle, was W. Brockman Boyce.

"Put it down, Brock, and raise your hands. You're under arrest," Drake said. "Don't make me do this."

Boyce looked up slowly. He had a faraway look in his eyes. "He has to die. They all have to die. There's no Santa Claus. He's pretending there is. Making them pretend. That picture this morning. You helped me find him," he said, holding the hypodermic needle in a fist in his hand. "There never was a Santa Claus. It's all a hoax. My parents said so. It's why I never got anything for Christmas. I have to stop him before he disappoints more children. I have to do this. I have to."

He raised his hand to jab Kerstman in the neck just before Drake and Barrie fired.

⁓ ⁓ ⁓

It was just before midnight on Christmas Eve and Dana was asleep. Finally. Drake and Shelly were in bed, having finished putting all the gifts under the Christmas tree, which dominated the front window of their living room. They left the tree lights on and the entire room twinkled in red, green, blue and yellow.

It was wonderful inside and it was made all the more magical because of the falling snow outside. The forecast called for six inches overnight.

Drake, who checked the door locks before coming to bed, reached over, turned off the light and pulled Shelly into an embrace. "I feel so bad. I really tried to find that doll. It kills me that she'll wake up in the morning and be disappointed."

With Shelly's head resting on his chest, Drake could feel her warm breath through his pajama top. "She'll get over it. We all do. You did the best you could."

༄༅ ༄༅ ༄༅

"Mommy, Daddy, wake up. Santa Claus came. Santa Claus came."

Dana's excited announcement stirred both parents awake. Drake rolled to his right and looked at the clock.

6:08.

He sat up and stretched his back before standing. His breath tasted like he had eaten dirty gym socks. He grabbed his robe and they headed downstairs. As they reached the living room, Dana came running back, a doll in hand.

"See, Mommy, see. I got it. Just like I wanted," the child said excitedly.

Shelly looked astonished as she took the doll from her daughter. She turned to Drake, "I thought you said you didn't get…"

Drake, his mouth wide open, wasn't paying attention to her. His attention was on the far right side of the Christmas tree, where, propped up against the wall, was a four-foot plastic Santa, exactly like the one he had smashed.

Zombie-like, Drake walked over to the Santa. A white note card was attached. The handwriting was in gold.

I thought you could use a new one for your roof. And thanks for the rescue.

Santa

Christmas Toffee Bars

2/3 cup shortening (Crisco)

2 cups brown sugar

1 cup white sugar

2 eggs

2 cups flour

1 teaspoon salt

1 teaspoon baking soda

1 teaspoon vanilla extract

1 cup chocolate chips

1 cup toffee bits

Red or green piping icing (optional)

Preheat the oven to 350°F.

Cream shortening and sugars. Add eggs one at a time until smooth.

Sift together flour, salt and soda, then add to the bowl. Add vanilla and mix until just combined. Fold in chocolate chips and toffee bits.

Spread in a 10-inch lightly greased square pan and bake for 30 to 35 minutes or until golden brown.

Cool in pan. Cut into bars (1 x 2.5-inch) and pipe "Noel", "Santa" or family names on each bar using red or green icing.

— *Recipe courtesy of Jane Turner*

Unexpected Gifts

By Stephen Terrell

h, baby, baby, baby! ! ! Momma's gotta pee."

Maria Wafford pushed her foot harder on the brake pedal and pulled her knees closer together. She held her breath. If something didn't move soon, she was going to pee all over the heated white leather seats in her new Mercedes sedan.

Johnny Mathis came over the seasonal satellite radio channel singing something about marshmallows and Christmas. Maria tried to sing along to get her mind off the intense urge in her bladder, but she couldn't concentrate enough to follow the words.

"Hurry up. Please!" The unhearing line of cars creeped forward a car length, then two. Then stopped.

Maria glanced into her rearview mirror. Her new dress hung from the hook above the window. Piled on the rear seats were nearly a dozen bags from Keystone at the Crossing—Nordstrom, Ann Taylor, Brooks Brothers, Michael Kors, Coach, and her favorite, Tiffany's. *Carter will be so happy with what he bought me for Christmas.*

One of the Nordstrom bags included the three new pairs of shoes she bought because she couldn't make up her mind which one went best with her new holiday dress.

Why didn't I just grab the first pair of shoes? I would be home now. I wouldn't be sitting here trying not to pee my pants.

A more urgent pang hit. "Oh, baby, why did I have to try on all those shoes? Why didn't I go before we left the store?"

Flashing blue and red lights reflected off the cars in the left lane. The lanes in front of Maria were clear. There was an exit just a short distance ahead. Hope sprang in her that she might make it.

Maria remembered the fake cover she had on her elementary school English book. "*Fifty Steps to the Outhouse, by Willie Makeit, Illustrated by Betty Wont.*" She gave a short laugh but stopped when she felt the increased pressure on her bladder.

The cars in Maria's lane were moving again, this time no longer creeping. Two minutes later, the right lane expanded into an exit. It wasn't an exit with which she was familiar, but from the roadside signs, she knew there were at least two gas stations. And bathrooms. *Thank Jesus, bathrooms.*

Maria accelerated down the exit, barely slowing to take the right turn at the bottom of the ramp. The neon sign of an off-brand gas station shined bright only a block away. She didn't even care if the bathroom was clean. She didn't care if she had to hover. She didn't even care if she had to use the sink. She just needed someplace to pee.

A handicapped space was closest to the gas station convenience store entrance. Maria saw the sign but ignored it. There was no time to deal with the car seat in the back. "Baby, momma's gotta pee. I'll just be gone a couple of minutes."

Maria left the car running to keep it warm and ran, nearly knocking over an elderly man exiting the store with two six packs in his hands.

"Hey, lady!"

Maria ignored him. "Bathroom!" she yelled at the young woman behind the counter.

The clerk rolled her eyes and pointed to a far corner of the store. A sign painted on the wall said "RESTROOMS." Maria ran, trying hold her legs together and not pee on the floor.

ᴄᴉᴗ ᴄᴉᴗ ᴄᴉᴗ

Kevan Johnson and Cedrick Stone stood behind some bushes in the shadows around the corner of the convenience store. The location gave them a clear view of the parking lot but kept them hidden from customers and any roving patrol cars. For the past hour they had been passing fattys and watching for the right opportunity to boost a car. It was Kevan who saw the gleaming luxury sedan pull into a handicapped spot, and a well-dressed woman get out and run into the store. The car was running.

Kevan punched Cedrick on the shoulder, then pointed. "Damn man, look what rolled in. That's an S Class. That's a hundred large if it's a dime."

Cedrick took a deep drag on the last bit of the joint, then threw the roach under a bush. "I don't know man. They got all kinds of theft stuff on them. They'll get us before we can get rid of it."

"She ran back toward the bathroom. She didn't have her purse with her, so I bet she don't got her phone, neither. We'll be clear across town before the cops get here. Let's do it."

If they hadn't split a shoplifted six-pack and shared three fattys, their decision might have been different. But for two seventeen-year-olds, the booze and bud took away any lingering inhibitions.

The looked at each other. Kevan nodded, and they took off on a run toward the car. They moved with an efficiency honed through a dozen earlier car thefts. Cedrick headed toward the driver's side, while Kevan ran behind the car. He slipped a magnetic dealer's plate from under his coat and slapped it over the existing plate. By the time Kevan reached the passenger seat, Cedrick already had the car in reverse and moving. Kevan grabbed the purse off the passenger seat as he slid into place.

"Go."

The car was up the entrance ramp and on the interstate before Maria stepped out of the store.

⁓ ⁓ ⁓

"Where's my car?" Maria said the words out loud. She scanned the lot, looking left, then right. *This is where I parked, isn't it? I put the car in park, didn't I?*

It took the better part of a minute for the reality to hit her. Her car was gone.

An instant later, Maria's world crashed around her. "My baby! Someone took my baby!"

She reached in her pocket, desperately grabbing for the cell phone that wasn't there. Panic shot through her like an electrical current. She ran back inside the store. She could barely get the words out through her gasps and sobs.

"Someone took my car! My baby's in it. My baby!"

The clerk stared blankly at Maria.

"Call the police. Someone took my car and my baby is in it. Call the police."

The clerk seemed only to vaguely grasp the gravity of the situation. With no discernable urgency, she walked to the end of the counter, picked up a desk phone and dialed 911.

⁓ ⁓ ⁓

Cedrick swung the car up onto the entrance ramp for I-465, trying to put as much distance as possible between them and the gas station. It would take the police at least ten minutes, probably longer, to respond to the 911 call for a stolen car. By that time, they could be halfway across Indianapolis. Maybe further.

"Jackpot!"

Cedrick looked over toward Kevan. He was holding up a thick wad of bills.

"How much?"

Kevan counted, then recounted. "Damn, there's more than $800 here. She had five hundies hid away in a side pocket. Plus there's five, no, six credit cards. There's a black American Express card, a black Visa card, one from Nordstrom's. These are top of the line. And we got her driver's license."

"Jackpot is right."

"Wait. We got pin numbers. She had 'em on a piece of paper in that side pocket. We are gold, man."

Cedrick and Kevan bumped fists and laughed. Cedrick nodded toward the console between them where an iPhone sat plugged into a charger. "Throw that out the window."

"We can get some money for that."

"They can track those. Get rid of it."

Kevan shrugged and grabbed the phone. Cedrick took the Washington Street exit. Kevan lowered his window a few inches and flipped the phone outside. In the mirror, he saw it bounce and shatter on the pavement.

"Cars like this. Don't they have trackers, too?"

Cedrick nodded. "That's why we're going right to Tony. He'll disable whatever they got. Cars like this, he sells them down in Mexico. That's what I heard. I bet he'll give us twenty bills for it."

"Sweet." Kevan turned to look at the back seat. "Hey, looks like she just did her Christmas shopping tonight."

"Anything in those bags worth having?"

"There ain't no Walmart bags here. Nordstrom. Brooks Brothers. Damn, there's even a Tiffany's bag. That's a jewelry store, ain't it?"

Kevan pulled the largest bag into the front seat. As he did, he heard a sound.

Cedrick heard it too.

It was cooing. It sounded like a baby.

Kevan moved the bags around revealing a car seat that had been blocked from view. "There's a baby back here. Oh, damn. There is a baby."

"What? You sure." As soon as he said it, Cedrick realized how stupid the comment was.

"Of course, I'm sure. I know what a baby is." Kevan twisted further in his seat to get a better look. Strapped inside the car seat, facing the rear, was a baby wearing a blue hooded winter coat with a blanket wrapped snugly around him. A pair of deep brown eyes looked up at Kevan, then closed in sleep.

Cedrick turned full around, catching a glimpse of the baby.

"Watch where you're going, Ced! You just ran that light."

Cedrick drove on for several blocks. When he saw an unlit parking lot in front of a deserted strip center, he pulled in and stopped.

"What are we gonna do, man?" There was an edge of panic in Kevan's voice. "Boosting a car is one thing, but taking a baby? They'll put us away for fifty years."

"I'm thinking. I'm thinking."

⁓ ⁓ ⁓

The store clerk called 911. It was fifteen minutes before the IMPD patrol car arrived. Maria was shaking. When she could catch her breath between sobs, she was cursing the police for taking so much time. It took another ten minutes for patrolwoman Karla House-man to calm Maria enough to get the basics of what had happened.

Maria provided very little in the way of a description of the car other than it was a new white Mercedes, one of the expensive ones. "S Class or C Class. I never can keep that straight." Neither she nor the clerk had seen anyone approach the car. It would be up to the detectives to check the store security video.

Karla radioed for detectives, then tried to calm Maria with little success. They walked to the police cruiser where Karla used the computer to check motor vehicle records. She confirmed that Karla's car was an S Class Mercedes sedan and obtained the license number. With all the information in hand, Karla radioed to request an immediate Amber Alert. By the time the detectives arrived and the Amber Alert was issued, nearly an hour had elapsed.

ᘓᑊᔋ ᘓᑊᔋ ᘓᑊᔋ

After several minutes of silence, it was Kevan who spoke. "We gotta get this car off the street."

"Tony's garage isn't far from here. We can take the back streets. He'll take this off our hands. Maybe he can loan us a car for a couple of days, too."

"But what about the kid?"

"We'll figure it out. But we gotta get rid of this car."

On the way to Tony's, they hit three ATMs. Using care to make sure their faces weren't caught by the security cameras, they used the cards and pin numbers from Maria's purse to drain $3,000 from her accounts. They split the money.

Fifteen minutes later, Cedrick drove the Mercedes down an unlit alley in an area of largely abandoned commercial buildings. He stopped in front of a ramshackle concrete block building with an oversized garage door. Cedrick blew the horn in two sets of three long bursts. It was a signal they had used before. With a clanking of metal on metal, the door slowly raised. As soon as the door was high enough to clear the roof, Cedrick pulled forward into the dim grease-stained garage.

Tony Wells walked toward them, wiping his hands on a shop towel. Nearly 60, short and round, wearing oil-stained coveralls, he was a throwback to another time when cars and life were less complex. Behind him, two men noisily worked under a late model Honda CRV that was up on a lift.

As Cedrick and Kevan got out of the car, Tony gave a low whistle. "Damn, where'd you boys pick that up?"

"Gas station," Cedrick said. "Woman went in and left the car running."

"S Class. Looks cherry."

"It is," Cedrick said. "But we got a problem." Cedrick opened the back door, revealing the car seat. The racket in the garage woke the baby, who began to fuss.

Tony stepped back like he had been punched in the chest. He waived his open hands at arm's length as if trying to ward off an apparition. "No, no, no, no. I'm not touching this. I ain't getting involved in nothing to do with snatching a kid."

"Com'on Tony," Cedrick said, a touch of pleading in his voice. "We'll take care of the kid. We ain't gonna hurt him. But this car's worth six figures. We can't just give it back. We'll even take a discount. You just give us one of your junkers so we can get back home, then you can pay us later after you off-load this."

Tony seemed to reconsider, then again shook his head. "I've been handling hot cars for forty years, but I don't touch nothin' else. No drugs. No violence. No snatching kids. That's how I stay out of jail and alive. I want you two out of here. Now."

Kevan and Cedrick looked at each other. Their dreams of a twenty-grand score were gone. Cedrick ran a hand through his hair. There was desperation in his voice. "Man, at least let us use one of your cars. We've brought you some good business. You can do that.

We'll dump the Mercedes someplace on the way home."

Tony stood with his hands resting on his ample belly, looking upward. After a long minute, he walked over to a pegboard loaded with maybe twenty sets of keys. Using his shop towel, he removed a set of keys from the board, wiped them down, then flipped them to Cedrick. "There's a piece of junk silver Caravan parked on the street about half a block down. Dinged up right side. You take it, but you were never here. You understand? You get caught, you heisted it off the street."

"Sure, Tony. Thanks."

"I'm serious. You were never here. And make sure you don't leave that Mercedes anyplace close to here."

Without another word, Cedrick and Kevan got back in the Mercedes and backed out of the garage. The Caravan was easy to spot. Kevan got out and slid behind the wheel. It smelled like three-day-old puke, but there wasn't going to be an Amber Alert for it.

Kevan followed the Mercedes through a series of two-lane residential side streets. Two miles from Tony's garage, Cedrick pulled the Mercedes behind a dilapidated commercial building with a fading sign for what had once been a local hardware store. Kevan put the van in park, but kept the engine running, afraid that if he shut it off, it might not restart. He watched Cedrick moving around inside the Mercedes. After several minutes, Cedrick got out carrying a small bag in one hand.

Kevan exited the battered Caravan and walked up to Cedrick. They stood in the dark among the rubble from the building. It smelled like piss and spoiled food, the remnants from the homeless vagrants and crack whores who had found a night's shelter in the lee of the building.

"What do we do now?" Kevan asked.

"We got almost $4,000 cash. And I grabbed this." Cedrick held up the Tiffany's bag in his hand. "It's a Rolex. We ain't getting twenty thousand for the car, but it ain't bad for one night. I wiped down the car. We just leave it here."

"What about the kid?"

"What about him? We didn't leave him in the car. The mother did. Let her worry about that. I ain't doing time 'cause some mom left a kid in a running car. That's on her."

"I don't know, Ced. It's just a baby. It's cold out here. Gonna get colder tonight. That kid might freeze to death."

Cedrick walked close to Kevan, their faces separated only by inches. "I told you, that's not my problem. If the mom didn't care, why should I. If the cops don't find that baby in time, it ain't my problem, neither. I didn't cause 'em to be so stupid."

Kevan looked down and shook his head. There was a long silence before he spoke. "I ain't leavin' no baby to die in the cold."

"Don't be a pussy, Kevan."

Kevan looked up. "I ain't a pussy. But I ain't no baby killer, neither."

Cedrick walked past Kevan and got into the driver's seat of the Caravan. "I'm leaving. You comin'?"

Kevan just stood there, his chin tucked into his chest. He heard the van slip into gear and drive away. He did not look up.

⁓ ⁓ ⁓

Maria sat in her living room, her face buried in her hands. There were no tears. She had cried them all out. Her husband, Carter, paced across the expansive formal living room. He had been doing so for the past two hours, ever since the policewoman brought Maria home. Two couples, friends who lived nearby, kept a silent vigil.

Karla Houseman, notebook open, sat in a straight-back chair that was carried in from the adjoining dining room. The detective in charge ordered her to drive Maria home and stay until someone arrived to relieve her.

Karla stood by as Maria broke the news to her husband. Carter Wafford responded first with disbelief, then shock, and finally with unrestrained anger. "How could you be so stupid? What kind of mother leaves her baby in the car with the engine running? Don't you have any brains at all? If anything happens to him, it will all be your fault." It was ugly.

As time passed, Carter made some effort to control his anger. He even made a meager effort to console his distraught wife. But there was no consoling her.

Karla couldn't help but think how awful it would be if the child was found dead. It would taint every Christmas for Maria and her husband for as long as they lived. It would undoubtedly destroy their marriage, if it had not already done so.

The ring of Karla's cell phone went through the room like a shockwave. Karla dug the phone from her utility belt. "Houseman."

Karla listened for several minutes. "Thank you. Keep me posted." She clicked off and turned to face the tense looks of everyone in the room.

"They found the car." Karla could see the instantaneous relief on the faces but knew it would not last. "Your baby wasn't there."

"Oh, Jesus." It was one of the neighbors.

Karla tried to provide some optimism. "There's some good news. There was no sign of violence. The car seat is gone. You said there was a blanket in the backseat?"

Maria nodded.

"It's gone, too. So is the diaper bag. Those are good signs. Someone is at least looking after the baby. The detectives and crime scene guys are there checking over the car. Patrolmen are out banging on doors, waking people up to see if anyone saw something. We've got all our resources on this." After a pause, Karla added, "We'll find your baby and bring him home."

Karla wished she felt more confident in what she was saying.

∾∾ ∾∾ ∾∾

Kevan walked through the night chill, aimlessly wandering along a cracked sidewalk in some nameless neighborhood. Kevan had lost track of how long he had been walking, or where he was. His right arm was numb from carrying the car seat. Under the blanket, with a winter coat snugly in place, the baby was asleep. Kevan didn't want to risk waking the baby by switching arms, so on he walked.

Solitary tears slid down his cheeks. He told himself they were from the wind in his face. Someplace inside, he knew better.

As he approached an intersection, he saw dim lights streaming from the windows in a large building. At first, he thought it was some type of warehouse. It was only as he drew closer that he recognized it as one of those old-fashioned churches—deep red brick with a bell tower stretching upward into the darkness. Concrete steps led to an arched entrance with two oversized wooden doors. From inside, there was a faint sound of music. He heard an organ, then a choir with the strains of a Christmas carol he had heard in childhood but didn't remember.

Kevan stopped and listened for a moment. He looked at the baby resting in the car seat, then headed up the steps. He eased open one of the doors that creaked ever so slightly. Light projected through the church from the front where the choir was singing. Kevan stood behind the last row of pews as music continued. A soloist was singing:

Mary did you know that your baby boy is heaven's perfect Lamb?
This sleeping child you're holding is the great I Am

The choir repeated the refrain "Mary did you know?" until the music faded. It was only then that the woman conducting noticed the stranger.

"Can I help you," she said, her voice carrying to the back of the church. When there was no response, the woman repeated her call.

Kevan said nothing, but his sobs became audible, echoing through the sanctuary. Patricia Holmes put down her conducting baton. She signaled the choir to stay in place and walked the length of the church to where Kevan stood, shoulders slumped.

Patricia tried to make her voice soothing. "I'm Reverend Patricia Holmes. Everyone just calls me Patricia." She looked at the car seat Kevan was holding. "What have we here? A baby?"

Slowly, Patricia leaned down and eased back the blanket. A baby with dark brown eyes, a full head of wiry black hair and deep cocoa-colored skin looked back, just a hint of a smile on his face. It was obvious that the child did not belong to the young ruddy-skinned teenager standing in front of her.

"He's so precious. What's his name?"

Kevan could barely get the words out. "I…don't know."

Patricia took the car seat from Kevan and eased the diaper bag off his shoulder. She directed him to a seat in the nearest pew. "Come sit. How did we sound? This is our last practice for our Christmas Eve program tomorrow night. That's why we're here so late. We just want to make it perfect."

Kevan nodded. "Pretty good, I guess," he mumbled.

Patricia turned toward the choir. She raised her voice to be heard. "That sounded wonderful. I think we're ready. I'm going to talk to this young man for a while, but I think we can call it a night. Thank you all. I'll see you tomorrow."

The choir began to mill about, putting on their coats. But no one left. They would not leave the pastor alone with this stranger who just wandered in.

Patricia sat next to Kevan. Her voice was now soft. "Why don't you tell me what's going on?"

So Kevan did. He told the entire story, only leaving out Cedrick's name and the visit to Tony's garage.

Patricia put her arm around Kevan as he talked. When he was done, they sat silent for a long time. Finally, Patricia said, "You did the right thing, you know that? Not hurting the child, I mean."

Kevan gave a small nod.

"You need to be proud of that. But we need to get in touch with the child's mother. She must be worried sick."

Kevan nodded again.

They sat in silence for several more minutes. Patricia nodded toward the front of the church where a nativity was set up near the alter. "You know why we celebrate Christmas don't you?"

"Yeah, I guess. I seen the stuff on TV."

"We celebrate the birth of a baby, much like this baby. That baby came to us to bring peace, to forgive us and save us from our sins."

A small tear ran down Kevan's cheek, but he said nothing.

"I think maybe that's what this baby has done, Kevan. Just like Jesus, this baby touched you. Touched those good places in you." She paused. "I think this baby is here to save you."

Tears flooded down Kevan's face. He made no effort to wipe them aside. "I ain't nothing but a doper and a thief. That's all I am."

Patricia gave Kevan a long hug, then whispered in his ear. "You know, the last man Jesus saved while he was on the cross was a thief."

Patricia stood. She slung the diaper bag over her shoulder and picked up the baby. "There's a changing table in the restroom. Let me change this child's diaper, then we can make some phone calls and get this baby back with his mother. I'll be right back."

Kevan nodded but didn't say anything.

Five minutes later, Patricia walked back into the sanctuary, the freshly-diapered baby nestled in her arms.

She looked out across the pews.

The church was empty.

Momma's Gotta Pea Soup

2 tablespoons butter

2 medium onions, chopped

2 large celery ribs, including leaves, chopped

2 large carrots, peeled and diced

1/4 teaspoon dried thyme and/or marjoram

1 1/2 to 2 pounds smoked ham hocks

2 cups dried split green peas

6 cups low low-sodium chicken broth & 2 cups water (or 8 cups water)

2 large bay leaves

1 beef bouillon cube

1 teaspoon salt

1/2 teaspoon black pepper

(optional) pinch of ground cayenne pepper

Melt butter in heavy large pot or Dutch oven over medium-high heat. Add onion, celery and carrots. Sauté until vegetables soften. Add thyme and/or marjoram; stir 1 minute. Add smoked ham hocks, split peas, then water / broth, bay leaves, bouillon, salt, black pepper, and cayenne pepper (if desired). Bring to boil. Reduce heat to medium-low. Partially cover pot; simmer soup until peas are falling apart, stirring often, about 1 to 1 1/2 hours, being careful not to allow soup to scorch.

Transfer hocks to bowl. Puree some or all of soup for smoother texture. Removed meat from hocks, dice and return to soup. Taste and adjust seasoning. Even better the second day.

CONTRIBUTOR BIOGRAPHIES

Joan Bruce is a pseudonym for D. B. Reddick, a short story writer with a dozen published stories to his credit. He is a former newspaper reporter/editor who worked at three daily papers in his native Canada before moving to the United States to become a college journalism instructor. He also worked two dozen years in the insurance industry. Reddick is now an American citizen and lives with his wife Rebecca in Camby, Indiana.

J. Paul Burroughs is a former teacher retired from the Indianapolis Public Schools. He and his wife, Ronda, live in Greenfield, Indiana with their adorable pug, Pip. He is currently working on a paranormal mystery series, *Karma and Crime*, a second series, *Dead and Circuses*, about a traveling circus in the 1850's, and further novellas on the adventures of Nick Mahoney, PI introduced in this anthology. *The Reindeer Murder Case* is his light-hearted look at the Noir genre set in the post war era of the late 1940's.

Ross Carley has been a military intelligence officer and an engineering professor. He is a cybersecurity consultant. His novels feature Wolf Ruger, an Iraq vet with PTSD, who is a private investigator specializing in cybercrime. Wolf solves murders and cybercrimes, undeterred by beautiful women and organized crime: *Dead Drive* is a private investigator murder mystery. *Formula Murder* is set in the fast-paced racing industry. *Cyberkill*, is a cyberthriller featuring casino hacking in Las Vegas, a cybercrime network in Chicago, and high-stakes cybermurder in Indianapolis.

Diana Catt has sixteen short stories in multiple genres in anthologies published by Blue River Press, Red Coyote Press, Pill Hill Press, Wolfmont Press, The Four Horseman Press, and SpeedCity Press. She was co-editor of *The Fine Art of Murder*. Her collection, *Below the Line*, is available now. She's an environmental microbiologist living and working in Morgan County, Indiana.

MB Dabney is an award-winning journalist whose writing has appeared in numerous local and national publications. He spent two decades as a reporter in Philadelphia, working first for *Business Week* magazine as a business correspondent and later for United Press International and the Associated Press. As an editor at *The Philadelphia Tribune*, the nation's oldest continuously published African -American newspaper, Michael earned national and state awards for his editorial writing. He lives in Indianapolis with his wife, two daughters, and dog Pluto.

Lori Rader-Day was the recipient of the prestigious 2017 Eugene & Marilyn Glick Indiana Authors Regional Award. She is the author of the Anthony Award-winning debut mystery *The Black Hour*, the Mary Higgins Clark Award-winning mystery *Little Pretty Things, The Day I Died* (2018 Anthony recipient, and a nominee for the Mary Higgins Clark, Thriller, and Barry Awards), and *Under a Dark Sky*. Lori is a member of Speed City Indiana Sisters in Crime as well as the Chicagoland Chapter of Sisters in Crime, the Midwest Chapter of Mystery Writers of America, and International Thriller Writers. In September she became the Vice President of Sisters in Crime National. She lives in Chicago, where she is the co-chair of the mystery reader conference Murder and Mayhem in Chicago.

Marianne Halbert is an attorney from central Indiana. Her horror, crime, and weird speculative fiction stories have appeared in magazines such as *Necrotic Tissue, Midnight Screaming*, and *ThugLit*, as well as in anthologies by Blue River Press, The Four Horsemen, Great Old Ones Publishing, Mystery and Horror LLC, Evil Jester Press, Mocha Memoirs Press, Grinning Skull Press, The Horror Society, and more. She prefers quiet, psychological horror in the vein of Shirley Jackson and Rod Serling. Marianne has been a panelist at AnthoCon and NECon. She is currently working on her ghost story novel *The Lady's Pocket*. Her work, including her collection *Wake Up and Smell the Creepy*, is available now.

B. K. Hart is an American Writer of humor, mystery, and horror. Short stories have seen publication in mystery anthologies with Speed City Indiana Sisters in Crime and in several independent horror anthologies. B. K. currently resides in Indiana.

Shari Held is an Indianapolis-based freelance journalist. She began her professional career at the age of sixteen writing a column for the *Greensburg Daily News*. More recently, she narrated Indianapolis: *A Photographic Portrait* and authored several For Dummies custom publications. Her first mystery story, *Pride and Patience*, appeared in the Sisters in Crime anthology *The Fine Art of Murder*. A Hoosier, through and through, Shari earned her Bachelor's degree (double major in English and History) from Purdue and worked toward her Master's degree at the Indiana University School of Journalism.

Elizabeth Perona is the father/daughter writing team of Tony Perona and Liz Dombrosky. Tony is the author of the Nick Bertetto mystery series, the standalone thriller *The Final Mayan Prophecy*, and co-editor of the anthologies *Racing Can Be Murder* and *Hoosier Hoops & Hijinks*. Tony is a member of Mystery Writers of America and Sisters-in-Crime. Liz Dombrosky graduated from Ball State University in the Honors College with a degree in teaching. She is currently a stay-at-home mom and preschool teacher. She also is a member of Mystery Writers of America and Sisters-in-Crime.

C. L. Shore began reading mysteries in the second grade, and has been a fan of the genre ever since. *Maiden Murders*, a prequel to A Murder in May, is her most recent release. Her short stories have appeared in Sisters in Crime anthologies and *Kings River Life Magazine*. Shore has been a member of Sisters in Crime for over a decade. A nurse practitioner and researcher, she's published numerous articles on family coping with epilepsy as Cheryl P. Shore. Shore enjoys travel and entertains a fantasy of living in Ireland for a year.

Stephen Terrell is an Indianapolis attorney and writer. He is the author of two legal thrillers, *Stars Fall* and *The First Rule*, and the short story collection *Visiting Hours and Other Stories form the Heart*, featuring the award-winning story "Visiting Hours." He contributed two short stories ("Street Art" and "Expose Yourself to Art") to the Speed City Sisters in Crime anthology *The Fine Art of Murder*. An avid motorcyclist and photographer, Stephen also authored a very personal photo-journal account of his last motorcycle trip with his longtime riding companion, *There and Back: Journal of a Last Motorcycle Ride*.

Janet Williams has been writing her entire life, first as a child making her own books and later as a journalist for newspapers in Pittsburgh and Indianapolis. She has always believed that journalism is, at its heart, strong storytelling. Today, she uses her experiences covering courts, crime, and politics to create her fiction. Since retiring from a corporate job in 2015, Janet has been teaching, writing, and hanging out with her dog, Roxy.

T. C. Winters owned a small business in the real estate industry for decades before deciding a change was required to preserve her sense of humor. She joined the Indiana chapter of the Romance Writers of America and the Speed City Sisters in Crime where she spent years studying the writing craft, specializing in humor and suspense. She is a resident of Central Indiana and enjoys cooking and gardening. Other loves include animals and canned cheese. Don't judge!